LEGEND OF THE SILVER DAWN

WRITTEN AND ILLUSTRATED
BY
VAANATHI CHONACHALAM

ISBN-13: 978-1-7322216-0-4
ISBN-10:173222160X

*To all those writers inspiring people to
dream....*

TABLE OF CONTENTS

PROLOGUE

"Put away the sword, Neera."

Two girls stood on a balcony, surrounded by towering turrets. A large, full moon shone on them.

Neera sheathed the razor-sharp blade. "Fine. But who are they?"

The other girl, Meera, peered over the side of the rail. "Guests."

A salty sea breeze wafted through the air. "But, I don't think we know them."

"Do you think it has anything to do with our training? Aren't we starting tomorrow?" Neera's fingers fidgeted, still reaching for her sword.

"I suppose Mama and Papa have been so wrapped up with preparations for our training— they forgot that our birthday is tomorrow." Meera sighed.

"Well, they can't forget! We're turning thirteen!" Neera said. "Wait. What if we become rulers soon?"

"We will become rulers soon, what about that?" Meera turned to face her sister.

"Don't you think we'll fight over it, like Mama and Papa always do?" Neera squeezed the hilt of her sword.

"No! Of course, we will fight— that doesn't mean we're going to hate each other. See? Mama and Papa never hated each other!"

"That doesn't mean we won't." Her hands were gleaming red from holding her sword so hard.

"I tell you. We'll be good rulers, and we won't hate each other."

"Fine, we don't talk about it for now." Neera finally let go of the sword.

The two stood in silence for a moment, drinking in the fresh air.

Meera began to hum a song. "What is that?" Neera asked. "It's a song that I learned from a book."

Neera scoffed. "Books. Swords are better." Meera didn't bother arguing. Neera's beliefs were usually strong, and she would keep arguing until the other gave up.

"Well, look at the moon."

"It looks so…"

"Silver," Meera finished.

ONE

THE SHIPS

20 YEARS LATER...

Today is the day the Ships come.
Today is my chance.
Safra sat up in her bed. It was the day that everyone in
the village was anticipating.
The day of The Ship's arrival.
Every five years, The Ships, a group of five ships that
traveled to distant lands, came to her island village of
Erina to recruit new men and youths. Safra's
grandfather, who had once been recruited, had told
many stories of his adventures on The Ships, and her
dream was to do the same thing.

One of the most famous stories of his was about Silver Island, a legendary place that held a prized object that was rumored to grant wishes. The Ships had failed to find it for almost two decades, and this year, they were coming to Erina again. Safra wanted to go with them as a part of the crew, but girls were not deemed capable of being a sailor. They were expected to do household chores, not go on voyages. Most of her friends didn't seem to mind doing just that, but Safra was different. She loved to just sit on the cliff and dream about the voyages she would experience, and she had wonderful ideas of what the Silver Island would look like. But The Ships would only recruit men. She had to have the potential of being a sailor, even if they could only consider her.

Well, it was worth a shot, she thought. *After all, Grandpa has taught me a lot about sea warfare! I am 12 years old, after all.*

"Good morning, Safra!" Her grandfather called out.

"Good morning Grandpa," the twelve-year-old said and gave him a hug.

Safra's parents had died a long time ago trying to search for the Silver Island, and her grandpa had taken care of her and her brother ever since. All she had left was a small stone locket with a picture of her parents inside it. There was an identical one which belonged to her brother. Hers had blue stones, his red stones. She fingered it nostalgically, wishing that she could remember them. Her grandpa had always told her that they had found the lockets on the very same Silver Island, and that had sparked her curiosity even more.

"Are you planning to go to the cliff today?" he asked, his eyes twinkling.

"Why?"

"I heard that The Ships are coming this afternoon."

That was enough for her. Safra started running as fast as she could, out of her house and to the cliff, which had the best view of the ocean. The soft green grass felt like silk as she ran, and she finally reached the spot. Every time she visited the cliff, all of her worries seemed to melt away. The warm breeze soothed her, becoming a lullaby, and the blue horizon seemed extra bright.

She waited and waited, and did not budge from her spot.

She trembled in nervousness, the excitement was too much to bear, and she was becoming more impatient by the moment.

But then, she heard a horn blowing through the air. For a moment, Safra could not comprehend anything that was happening. She froze, until she realized The Ships were near.

She ran back to the village as fast as her legs could take her, the lump in her throat becoming bigger.

What if they don't recruit me? Shake the nerves off, Safra!

"The Ships are here! The Ships are HERE!" Safra shouted at the top of her lungs.

"They're here?" a familiar voice echoed. An olive-skinned, brown-eyed boy with untamed black hair sat on the porch.

"Ridan! There you are! Come on, let's go and wait for The Ships!" she called out to her brother.

Safra and Ridan looked like twins, although Ridan was younger by two years. They shared many of the same interests as well, such as a love for the ocean. But, Safra had more of an obsession with The Ships. Ridan mostly wanted to be a scientist, as he loved ocean wildlife, and loved studying it as well.

The two ran out onto the beach, the soft, moist sand squishing between their toes. They watched The Ships nearing the coast, their monstrous shapes looming over the water.

Safra became overwhelmed with thoughts and daydreams, her head filling with images of her future voyages.

The ships docked in the port, and they began unloading supplies and food. The Ships were a main supply of merchandise for Erina, and in return for that, the village would provide strong, resourceful men for The Ships.

"Safra… how about we come here tomorrow?"

She stared at him in utter shock.

"They're going to be here for another day. We can decide on what to say and come back, prepared. We need a game plan. You see, they might not have child recruitment," Ridan explained. Only a few groups of ships recruited young boys, and rarely girls.

"Hmmm… That makes sense..," Safra said with reluctance. *I want the adventures to start already!*

They stared at the gigantic sails of the marvelous Ships one last time before they ran back to their home. "Hello Grandpa," Safra said.

He put down his glasses. "Back already?" he asked, raising an eyebrow.

"We wanted to think of a plan," Ridan yelled as he walked into the kitchen.

Safra ran upstairs and went to her room, which had the perfect view of the port, where she saw them still unloading the supplies. *Tomorrow is the day,* she thought. *Tomorrow is the day my dream will come true.*

TWO

THE MISSION

The next morning, Ridan and Safra woke up early, and immediately raced to the port.

"Okay Ridan, you remember everything, right?" Safra asked. She was tense, sweating profusely.

"Yep. Just talk casual and play it cool," he said.

Safra took a deep breath, and approached a tall, young man in sailor attire.

"Ummm…Excuse me," Safra said.

"What do you want?" The sailor's grouchy voice seemed to intimidate Ridan, but Safra continued anyway.

"I was wondering….if we could join your crew. Do you have child recruitment?" Safra asked hopefully, but knew that she probably sounded like a fool.

Why am I doing this?

"What? Are you kidding me? Do you think two kids would be recruited? This isn't a joke," he laughed.

Safra was going to protest, but Ridan pulled her arm and said,

"C'mon Safra, let's go."

"But—" she stammered as Ridan dragged her away. When they came home, Safra felt betrayed. She had been so enthusiastic about The Ships, and now Ridan had pulled her back home. *Doesn't Ridan want to go on The Ships? Isn't he interested? Fine then, I'll have to do it myself,* she thought.

Then Ridan said, as if reading her mind, "Safra, I can explain."

"What? What? You don't want to go on The Ships, right? The Ships are leaving tonight! What's the big idea?!" Safra frowned.

"No! Saf, listen. He himself said children aren't allowed. There's nothing we can do. Calm down," he said slowly.

"So what?"

"We sneak onto the ship."

"What? Are you crazy? If we go, the guards will see us! And, plus, what if we fail?" Safra was shocked by her brother's plan. The thought of failure intimidated her like no other. It was something that always popped into her head whenever she had a task to complete.

"What if we sneak in at night, when nobody is guarding the ship?" Ridan's mouth curled up into an evil smile. Safra grinned, rubbing her hands together. She tried to look like she agreed. *Maybe it'll work.*

A few hours later, the sky had begun to darken, and Safra and Ridan were getting ready to execute their master plan. They took a satchel filled with some food, extra clothing, and water. They bid goodbye to their grandfather, knowing that if their plan succeeded, they might only see him after five years or longer.

"Go get 'em kids!" he said with a large smile, but he could not hold back his tears.

Safra glanced at a pocket-watch that her grandpa had given her for her tenth birthday. *No matter how far apart we will be, he will be with me.I have to take this with me.*

The two of them started walking to the rear entrance of the docked main ship, looking back at their grandfather again, making sure he was still there. Both of them were terrified that someone would catch them, so both remained silent, not exchanging a single word. The coast was clear, and they climbed up a small rope ladder into the ship.

Safra took a deep breath of relief. They had done it! Both of them dashed into a small storage room, and planned to stay there for the night. It had been an easy task, but they still had the danger of being discovered. "Let's eat," Ridan said, obviously happy as well.

Safra took a sandwich appreciatively, and fingered her locket. Ridan took his identical one in his hands. The thoughts of their parents filled their heads, images running through their minds. Blurry memories seemed to flash in front of them.

Then, a powerful light emerged from both of their lockets, Safra's blue, Ridan's red. They faded as soon as they came.

I have never seen that happen before! Their lockets then flickered with the same light, and looked like it was coming from the interior. With trembling hands, Safra opened her locket to see a black, obsidian stone shaped like an elephant sitting on top of the picture.Ridan copied her action, only his was shaped like a large animal's tooth.

Safra fell to the ground.

My eyes close, but I awoke in a different, beautiful place. It is cold and windy and covered in snow, and I have never seen such an island like this. Then I notice I am not alone. A ship is docked

When she finally opened her eyes, she could see that she was back in reality, inside the storage room.

"Safra! You just drifted off for a few seconds," Ridan said.

"Only a few seconds? Felt like a long time to me," she said.

"Wait…what?"

She explained what she had seen to Ridan, and he was astonished.

"The lockets probably had something to do with this. But for now, let's get a good night's sleep and then think about this. Good night," Ridan said, and then curled up in the corner of the room.

Safra wanted to find out more, but she was tired, and she had much bigger problems to face the next day.

"Good night, Ridan," she said, and drifted away into dreamland.

THREE

THE CAPTAIN

Safra woke up the next morning and checked her pocket-watch.

"Ridan, wake up! It's six forty -five! Wake up!"

"What…Huh?" Ridan got up from the floor.

"The sailors wake up at five o'clock. They could have caught us," Safra whispered quietly. Sounds of footsteps behind the door seemed to come closer and closer. Then the door creaked open!

"Oh no!"

A huge shadow of a man filled the doorway. The light shone through, showing his blue, beady eyes.

"Come over here everybody! Two kids snuck onto our ship!" the giant man boomed.

Safra's heart pounded in fear. In the darkness of the small room, she could not see Ridan's expression, although she could guess what it would be. She heard the screams and shouts of the sailors, demanding they should be brought to the Captain. Her imagination filled with horrid images of the two of them being tossed into the cold sea. The shouts became louder, and strong arms lifted them out of the room and onto the deck.

"Ah," Safra groaned as the bright beams of the sun hit her face.

The man who had made fun of them the other day was in the crowd of the sailors. Frowning, he said, "These two kids? They were at the town yesterday, guys! They wanted to be part of the crew!"

All the other men started chortling in scorn.

"The Captain doesn't need to know about this. We'll land in hot water for not taking security measures," one of them said.

"Yeah, we'll just throw 'em out for the sharks!"

They all snickered, and Ridan looked like he wanted to cry.

Finally, Safra could stand it no more.

"What do you think of yourselves? Huh? Laughing at a couple of kids like that!" She wanted to throw herself at them and tear them to tiny pieces. Silence filled the air. "What do you think you are? If you're so brave, then why didn't you find *Silver Island* yet?"

The sailors surprisingly did not respond. They looked terrified, and Safra found out why.

A tall man wearing a dark blue jacket and hat strutted out onto the dock. He had a handsome, rigid face with a small, shabby beard, and a large scar in the shape of three dark lines ran across a side of his face. She shivered in fear, wondering about the story behind it. She assumed he was the captain, and she could see why the sailors were scared of him.

He did not pay attention to Safra and Ridan, but he glanced at them for a moment before saying, "How could you let these kids on this ship? It is very dangerous." The sailors remained silent.

"At least, how could you let this little girl talk back to you? And she's mentioning Silver Island, as well. She has got some nerve, I tell you! And, I heard your entire conversation, by the way. You are all landing in 'hot water'. Now, I guess we've just got some extra junior janitors here," he said looking at Safra and Ridan dismissively.

"You have all been relieved of scrubbing the deck clean every morning," he said and laughed heartily, but nobody else seemed to have an intention of laughing back.

He snapped his fingers, and the two of them were dragged away. Safra expected them to be imprisoned somewhere, but instead they were lead to a study filled with maps, books, telescopes, and figurines. It had a vintage, old look to it. "This must be the captain's study," Ridan whispered.

"I wonder why he brought us here," Safra whispered back.

Safra then heard the sound of a door creaking open, but did not dare look. She knew it was the captain.

He walked into the room and sat down. He gave them a cold stare, scrutinizing them carefully.

"Why are you here?"

"Excuse me…But *what?*"

"Why are you here?" the Captain repeated slowly. "We came here to join the crew," Ridan spoke up, his courage slowly coming back.

"Okay, but what was all that *Silver Island* talk about? The Silver Island does not exist!"

Safra stood up. "It does! It does! You're lying!" Then she stood up in anger. "Grandpa told me! He told me that Silver Island exists!"

"Maybe your grandpa is just telling you some old stories that popped into his head," he said, rolling his eyes.

"My grandpa's name is Pierre C. Lewis, and he is a perfectly sane man."

"I knew him before! Does he still live there?"

"Just answer my question— Does Silver Island exist, or not?"

"Yes, it does, it does," he said. "I even saw the Silver Serpent's Cove once."

"Then why didn't you go there?" Safra asked.

Silver Serpent's Cove was a famous landmark which led to the island. It was rumored to be hidden very cleverly and you had to follow a very precise route to find it.

"Because…I was young," he said. "I did not know how valuable it was, and I did not note down what path I took," he sighed deeply.

"Then why aren't you trying to find it?"

"Haven't you heard of star paths? We tried thinking of all the routes! It has to be some of the smaller stars, because the bigger stars would be definitely too obvious!" He banged his fist on the table. "Sorry," he said, shaking his fist. "I am the Captain here. You are…"

"I'm Safra and he's Ridan. What's your name?"

"What?" He stared at Safra like she was an alien. "No, I mean, what's *your* actual name?"

He simply left the room without answering. He seemed very suspicious, and all of the sailors seemed terrified when he was around. She did not know what to think of him. Still in confusion, she and Ridan were escorted out of the room, and presented with a bucket of water and sponges.

"Scrub the deck," said a tall and chubby sailor.

Safra started cleaning, and she noticed that the sailor was still standing there.

"I'm Chuck, and I'm sorry everyone was laughing— I mean, I didn't laugh at you, and I just wanted to say that, I really like your grandpa— he was my hero." Safra looked up at him, waiting for him to say more.

"I couldn't help but eavesdrop— after all, I wouldn't blame you for wanting to be recruited."

"Well…Okay…Fine. Wait. Can you meet me at the main mast at midnight? Thanks," Safra said.

Chuck nodded, bewildered, and walked away. Ridan's face scrunched up. "What? Why did you tell him to do that?"

"Let's just say that I have a lot of questions," she replied. The day passed quite slowly. Safra and Ridan were sweating and breathing heavily after an hour of work, but there was much more to do. They could do nothing else but listen to the crew's commands, because they could do anything to the both of them.

They worked the whole day, but even though they only
got some water and a small plate of biscuits to eat, they
had breaks whenever they wanted, and Safra loved it.
Every ounce of the salty sea air, the blue waves, and the
beautiful skies made her smile.

But Ridan seemed to differ. "I haven't seen a single new
specimen of sea life here. At least at Erina there were
porpoises."

"Oh come on, Ridan. You always complained how
boring the porpoises were," Safra chuckled. "Humph,"
Ridan scoffed and walked away.

FOUR

ANOTHER VISION

Safra sighed. She ran out onto the figurehead, which was a large and beautiful falcon. She kneeled on the wings, and it provided her the best balance. She had always dreamed of doing this.

I close my eyes, and I feel like I have been whisked to a different land again, but it is nighttime and I am standing near the helm. A bright light distracts me. It's the star Polaris, the North Star, and the ship is heading towards a small cove that is sparkling like silver.I could see a route mapped on the sea.

It probably is the Silver Serpent's Cove! Overwhelmed by happiness, I suddenly feel like I'm floating on air. Then it fades again.

Safra felt someone tap her shoulder and whirled around, only to see Chuck.

"Lunch is served," he said.

Safra entered a small room with a bunch of sailors sitting in a circle around a sizzling pot of red liquid. *It smells like heaven,* Safra thought, and took a seat next to Ridan.

He did not speak to her, and the other sailors seemed to eye her in disgust. *They can't even say a good hello*, Safra thought. She decided to say something.

"Uh…This food is really good! Whoever…made it?" She looked around, an awkward smile creeping up on her face.

A thin, gangly man wearing dirty, stained overalls whirled around.

He said, "Thank you, um… Nobody ever says that to me. Thanks."

Safra smiled at him, but then noticed all the others frowning at her, including Ridan.

She just rolled her eyes and started eating her food again.

After lunch, she slowly caught up with Ridan. "Ridan! What's the matter? Why are you mad at me?"

"You and your silly ship stuff. I never wanted to come here anyway. You're always like 'Ships this, Ships that,' and Grandpa always told more stories when you wanted him to. Now we're stuck here!"

"But…But I saw the Cove in another vision thing. It is true," Safra said, trying to coax Ridan into believing her.

She still could not explain the visions. She knew it was the lockets, but why?

"I wish I never came with you!" Ridan stormed off.

"I never asked you to come!" Safra yelled after him.

She brushed it off. Ridan had been the one who insulted her. But now, no one trusted her except Chuck.

At midnight, Safra walked down to the mast, where Chuck was standing. "Okay, I called you here because I want to know the answers to a few questions," she said.

She went on to grill him about the Captain, her grandpa's past, Silver Island, the other sailors, and asked about the different paths that they had taken over the years.

In the end, she had got a lot of answers. But, there was nothing on the Captain. One piece of crucial information emerged: they had never followed the star path of The North Star, also known as Polaris. *Coincidental,* she thought.

Then, a brilliant idea clicked in her head. It was the only one that could turn this whole thing around, but she needed Ridan's help now. She ran back to the storage room where they were supposed to sleep, but she could not see Ridan.

"Ridan, where are you? Ridan, are you there?"

"Yes?"

She turned around to see Ridan staring at her. "Sneaking off at night, are you?" He sneered at her. "Yes, and I have a plan. Please… I need help."

"I don't have to help."

"Fine, have it your way. If you don't want to find Silver Island, don't help me," she said, taunting him.

Ridan hesitated. Safra knew he wanted to find Silver Island too.

"Come on Ridan, we have nothing to lose," she said slowly.

"Okay," he said, and smiled forcibly.

"All we have to do is find the engine room," she said. "Chuck told me where it is," Safra started walking towards a rusty door.

"Wait, what? Wait for me!" he yawned.

They walked down a small set of stairs and found another door, which led to the engine room, and Safra fumbled around to try to find the tool that increased the speed.

Luckily, her grandfather had taught her everything she
needed to know. She turned up the speed six knots.
"Okay, now we need to go and find the helm," Safra said.
"Why are we trying to turn the ship?" Ridan asked.
"You'll see," she replied.
They raced up the stairs to the dock, where the helm was.
"Ridan, you're going to steer the ship, okay?"
"What?"
"Just do it!" Safra shouted, and Ridan turned the helm to
the left, turning the ship slowly, and Safra could see the
North Star shining brightly over the night sky. She
directed him through the route she had seen in her
vision. "Perfect," she said, motioning for him to stop.
She thought she could see something in the distance, and
she knew that tomorrow morning they would be close
enough to see what it was.
 It was a brilliant sight, and both of them sat down,
mesmerized by the light. It had been a tiring day, so both
of them sat down near the helm and dozed off.
 Safra was exhausted, but she knew her plan would work.
She smiled to herself and settled down on the hard,
wooden floor.

FIVE

TROUBLE

The next morning, Safra woke up to a rough hand shaking her awake. Only one word jumped to her mind. Trouble.

"What the…These little kids steered our ship off course!" All of them gathered into a crowd and stared menacingly at Safra and Ridan.

"I knew they weren't to be trusted!"

"Wait. Everyone, listen!" Ridan stood up angrily. "What course? What course, huh? You all are…You're a bunch of sissies! You can't even find Silver Island! My parents died because of this island, and that's probably because they went alone. You have a group of five ships, and over 100 men! Why can't you just try harder?" Ridan let out a giant breath. All of the sailors remained quiet. Hearing all the noise, the Captain walked out from his study, a tough expression painted on his face, and he did not change it. Safra imagined his face to be glass.

Then, all the glass seemed to break.

"Look! Look! It's the Silver Serpent's Cove! Yes!" The
Captain smiled a broad smile and jumped for joy, as he
could see the cove in the far distance. It was the cove
from Safra's vision! "I found it! I found it!"
Safra gave the Captain a dismissive look.
"They found it! To Safra and Ridan!" He grinned. "To
Safra and Ridan!" Everyone chorused, and lifted them up
into the air.
For Safra, it was the best day of her life. They didn't have
to scrub the decks. They were finally part of the crew.
They were headed to the Serpent's Cove, and then to the
Silver Island. Everything seemed perfect.
"Safra!" she heard the Captain calling her.
"Yes, Captain," she said.
"Chuck told me you had a lot of questions, and I am the
perfect person to answer them. Shoot," he said and
smiled.
"You're saying I can ask you questions?" She noticed the
suspicious change in his attitude.
"Obviously, that's what I'm saying. Ask me," he said.
"Okay, first, Grandpa told me there was a legend to the
Silver Island, about it granting wishes. Tell me more," she
said.
"Okay, all right. The Silver Island was a big island in
which people lived. Only rich people could afford it, as
the silver sands on its beach were supposed to grant
wishes. Until, there was a huge storm, and half of the
island was washed away. The last of its sand was put into
a small pit inside a cave inside of the Mona, a big volcano.
People left, and nobody knew why, as it was still a large
island and it had perfect living conditions. But, suddenly,
it disappeared. It was hidden forever, by some weird
phenomenon, and only the Cove holds the secret to

finding it. There are mentions of some legend about a Silver Dawn." He stared out the window.

"There is so much more to this than I thought. Well, how did you know all this?" Safra asked.

"My father, a former captain and retired resident of Silver Island, was there during the storm, and he survived it. He died soon after that, and he left his journal to me. That is how I know." His eyes glistened, and Safra felt sorry for him as she knew how it felt to lose a parent.

"Any more questions?" he asked, drying his eyes.

"No, thank you for answering them though," Safra said awkwardly.

"I hope you don't mind me asking…Well… You were mentioning Ridan's parents…" he asked. Safra knew what he was talking about.

"First of all, Ridan is my brother. And my parents, well… They were looking for it because my aunt was living there. They wanted to find out why she moved out, and why nobody used the sand to wish the island to magically be rebuilt again. It was a mystery they wanted to solve," she said, "and they died because of another storm, soon after it disappeared."

"Oh…I'm sorry. Yes, yes, it is a mystery why nobody used the sands very much and why they hid it as well. I guess we will just have to wait until we get to the Cove. There are more secrets to it than you think. Good night, Safra."

"Good night, Captain."

Safra went to her cabin, where Ridan was waiting for her.

"Safra! Where were you?"

"I was asking the Captain some questions. You?" she asked.

"The helmsman, Tom, asked me if I could take over with steering the boat for a while. He taught me some more basics," he replied.

"That's good. The Captain told me about more about the Silver Island legend," said Safra excitedly.

"Safra, can I tell you something?"

"Yeah?"

"Don't trust the Captain too much. He's very secretive, and he has some books about Silver Island he refuses to show anyone else. Isn't that suspicious? We should be careful, so don't tell him anything you find out just yet," said Ridan.

"But— He seems nice. I mean, he gave me answers," she said, even though she was suspicious herself.

"Be careful, that's all I'm saying. We'll discuss our finds first before we tell him," he said.

Safra agreed, and she told him all about the legend that the Captain had told her, and they both did not understand that why the people of Silver Island didn't use the sand to wish the island back to normal, and why the people evacuated even though part of it was still intact. Still, Safra now knew that now her peculiar visions were reliable, but Ridan had yet to discover what he could do with his locket.

"Let's hope we reach the Cove soon," Ridan said. "Yeah! There could be so many new things, waiting to be discovered!" Safra said happily.

"New adventures await," Ridan said and smiled.

And as they thought, by the time they had woken up, they had reached the Cove. It looked more beautiful close up than from far away. Safra thought its shimmering rocks on the coast looked like pure silver, and even the gray, dismal sky fit the scene, as it looked somewhat desolate. The ship let down a rowboat in which the Captain, Safra, Ridan, and the sailor who had made fun of them back in Erina, Ahmed, rode to the cove. Ahmed was the Captain's most trusted crew member, and he did not seem to like the two of them. But for Safra, he did not matter at the moment. All she could see was the beautiful cove in front of her eyes. She sighed, content. She had finally gotten one step closer to her dream of finding Silver Island.

SIX

DANGER AND DISCOVERY

They reached shore, and Safra rushed out on the cool, wet sand. Further into the cove, she saw lush, green grass, with little pink blotches of flowers.

She was dazzled by the beautiful landscape, and started running. She looked back, noticing that Ridan was behind her, and she also could hear the Captain telling them to slow down, but she did not heed his warning.

She neared the center of the cove, where a wall of rocks stood in their way. There, she spotted a cliff with a cave on the top of a hill. "It must be the clue!" she exclaimed, and tested the wall with her fist. "It's rather brittle," she muttered, and several rocks crumbled down, perfect for her to fit through. She stepped through it, and all she saw was a black flash before a bone-breaking smash threw her on a rock on the other side of the Cove! She felt too dizzy to move.

"Safra!" Ridan shouted.

He could see a vicious-looking creature that looked like a hyena, except it was black. It stood guard next to Safra, and he knew that it wasn't moving any time soon.

Ridan started shouting at it to try and scare it away. "Go away! Go away," he said and waved his arms, standing behind the wall so it could not harm him.

Then his locket started glowing with bright red light, and then it faded. To his surprise the hideous monster ran away, and he figured it was because of the locket. He decided not think about it at the moment, and then he ran to help Safra. "I'm better now," she said. "Where is the Captain?"

"He must have run away when he saw the creatures," he said.

"What a coward," said Safra. "Ridan, what were you doing there? You were kind of, I don't know, making animal noises?"

"What? You mean…"

"Yeah, you were barking and snarling, and after that they ran away."

"But I was talking normally! But my locket glowed…Which means…" Ridan murmured. A train of thought rushed through his head.

"Okay, now let's go to that cave, it might have the clue inside it," Safra said

"But we need to watch out for those *things*," said Ridan.

"Yeah, yeah, we'll be fine," Safra rolled her eyes and walked on.

They climbed up a few boulders, and found a staircase carved into the rock, which led them to the cave.

As she entered, it felt like she was in another era, the rocky surface carved with drawings and ancient letters.

I close my eyes again, and this time, I am still in the cave.
But, I see a lady, and she is holding a stone plaque. She seems to
be looking for something, and she goes to the far corner of the cave
and touches a drawing of a beautiful woman, and it seems to click
in place.
A pillar rises from the ground, but stops halfway, and then
she places the plaque in the middle, and the pillar recedes back into
the ground.

Safra opened her eyes to see Ridan staring at her.
"Another vision, I guess?" He rolled his eyes. "Yes…This
time I think I saw the past…" she murmured.

Safra wandered to the corner of the cave, where the
drawing of the woman was. She was stunningly beautiful.
She seemed so familiar, yet so unlike anybody else Safra
had seen before. Her shiny brown hair fell in curls on her
shoulders, her beautiful hazel eyes shining in the light.
Underneath her drawing, there was one word:
'Meera'.

Safra assumed that it was her name. Safra raised her
hand to the wall, and pressed the drawing, on the
woman's hand. It clicked softly, and Safra jumped back in
shock as the lady's hand felt like soft skin. A tinkling
bracelet with a glimmering key on it hung from her wrist.
The drawing seemed to move, and she smiled wistfully at
Safra for a moment and then froze. The same pillar rose
up from the ground, holding a stone plaque and a rolled
up map.

Ridan stood there in shock.

Safra picked up the map from the ground, and unrolled it. In big letters in old-fashioned cursive, it said: Silver Island. Although it was an important find, she did not feel interested by the map.

Safra dropped it absentmindedly into Ridan's hands, and walked over to the pillar, where she picked up the stone plaque instead. It was covered in a peculiar language she could not understand.

"Ridan! Look at this!" Safra exclaimed.

Ridan examined the plaque, and ran his hand over the stone. Then his locket started glowing, and so did the script. Safra's eyes widened in surprise, as Ridan seemed to be reading it with ease, murmuring in a foreign tongue. He could read it!

"That's amazing! You can read and speak other languages! That explains you talking to those creatures!" Safra said.

When he took his hand off the plaque, it stopped glowing, and Ridan said, "I could understand it! It told me to rotate something on the bottom…"

"Someone's coming! Hide the plaque, in your satchel! Take the map!" Safra exclaimed in horror.

Ridan did as he was told, and they could hear the Captain shout, "Safra! Ridan! Where are you?"

He obviously had not noticed the cave. "Let's not show him the plaque, only the map," Safra said.

"Why?"

"You said we can't trust him," she said.

They raced down the stairs and down the boulders to see the Captain and Ahmed waiting for them.

"I was wondering where you were," he said, looking a little sheepish.

"Oh yeah? Then where were you when Ridan and I were attacked by that monster? Where were you then?" Safra felt herself suddenly getting angry. He had deserted them when they had needed him, and he hadn't even called for help.

"I'm…I'm sorry…Ooh, you both have discovered something! It's the clue!" he said, his eyes widening. He snatched the map from Ridan's hands, and unrolled it. "You two…You two are wonderful! We're going to Silver Island!" the Captain jumped for joy, and they immediately went back to the ship and set sail. Ahmed frowned and stomped away.

SEVEN

CELEBRATION

"Everyone, we're going to Silver Island!" The Captain said with a proud smile on his face.

Safra decided to brush off the incident and celebrate. It was a time to rejoice, not wallow in anger and sadness. Everyone danced and sang, and delicious food was cooked. Safra was having the time of her life, and even Ridan looked like he was having fun as well. She felt happy as she could see everyone smiling and talking to each other in perfect harmony. *Everyone should be like this every day,* she thought.

Soon she went to her cabin, where she flopped onto the bed. "I'm beat," she said to herself.

She wished Ridan was here, so that they could figure out more about the plaque. It was definitely linked to the drawing of Meera. The image was stuck in her mind, her long, twisted brown hair, her hazel eyes, and her elegant face— it was all so confusing and mysterious.

Safra shook it off, and decided to wait for Ridan, but she took it out anyway, just to look at it.

Her palm brushed the back of the plaque. Squiggly lines and markings were carved into it. *That does not look like a language, she thought. Hmmm…*

She rubbed her fingers against it, caressing it softly. Then the door burst open, and Safra scrambled to hide the plaque.

"Ridan! You scared me!" Safra said, narrowing her eyes. "Sorry! Whoo! That was such a party!" he shouted over the noise.

"I know! Isn't this fun? You know, everyone being happy, singing, dancing, the food— it's the best!"

"Yep," he nodded, closing the door.

"Ok, what did you read on the plaque?" Safra handed it to him.

"It told me to rotate the bottom part…" Ridan held the bottom of the stone and spun it, and it turned into two plaques, which were connected to each other. He separated them, and inside there was an old piece of paper stuck to the rock, and it was written in English. "Let's read it," said Safra.

Things are not what they seem to be,
And there are always hidden consequences.
Never believe what you see.
Although your hard work will not be in vain,
think before you leap.
Greed and desire only bring pain.
There is a limit— use it wisely and for good.
More than that will bring you down.
Do you think you would?

"Wow… this sounds ominous," Safra said.

"Do you think this is even real? Anyone could have made this up! Whatever," Ridan scoffed. It was certainly unlike him to jump to conclusions.

"Uh…Yeah! We should celebrate," Safra said, but she believed the poem, deep down. She had seen it in the vision, and she trusted herself. Safra lay there in her bunk. Was Silver Island a good idea? The plaque had talked about some consequences. What if there were rules? These sailors would never, ever follow them, even if they had any idea what they were. They would take all the silver sand, and use all of it.

Should I talk to the Captain? Safra mused, frustrated. But with the recent events that were happening, she did not feel like talking to him. He did not seem to care about them at all. They were the ones who had found the Cove, and they were the reason for the future discovery of Silver Island.

And, what was up with Ridan?

I'll think of something tomorrow, she thought.

That flicker of worry still remained, but she did her best to fall asleep quickly.

Don't think about it, she thought, but it clouded her mind. Who was Meera, and what was she trying to tell her? Questions swarmed through her head, but she suppressed them. She sighed and closed her eyes.

EIGHT

THE STORM

Safra woke up the next morning to a strong gust of wind blowing through her cabin. She sat up, and saw that Ridan was awake as well.

"What was that?" he shook his head.

"It's so…So cold," Safra shivered, and pulled her covers over her head.

"Let's see what's going on," Ridan said, and walked out on deck.

"It's early," she said, but Ridan had already disappeared.

"Safra, I think you should see this," he shouted from the deck. His voice seemed muffled.

She threw over the covers and followed him. A huge blast of wind knocked her off her feet! She could barely open her eyes. Drops of water started to land on deck.

"Captain! Captain!" she shouted , noticing that he was awake, trying to steer. The island was in sight!

"Hang on! I think we're entering a storm!" the Captain tried as hard as he could to steer the ship around, but he was thrown into the cargo hold by another gale.

"Steer it…Around. Oof!" he yelled.

Safra squinted to see a rope tied to the helm, hanging downwards. If she got ahold of the rope, she could reach the helm easily.

There was only one problem. Ahmed.

"Ahmed! Hand me the rope!" she shouted.

He hesitated. She knew that he was going to try and do it himself. It started to rain heavily, and she knew that he could not do it. The rope could hold her weight, but not Ahmed's. He scowled, and grabbed the rope. He tied it around his waist and proceeded to the helm. And, as she expected, the rope's strands loosened, but it was not too late.

"Ahmed! The rope is breaking! Hand it to me! Come on! You'll fall overboard!" she shouted, but in vain.

A bloodcurdling scream echoed through the air, and with a loud splash, Ahmed was gone.

"Yay! The grouch is gone," Ridan muttered sarcastically.

"Not the time to joke around! We've got to save him!"

Safra was now thankfully closer to the rope, and it was still long enough.

She tied it around her waist, and leaped off the side of the ship. She could see Ahmed flailing in the water, but he was getting farther and farther away.

"Grab my hand!" she shouted.

He heeded her command, and then grabbed the rope as well.

"Ridan, help us! Help! Pull us up!" she shouted. Unfortunately, Ridan did not seem to hear her.

"Ridan, come on over here!" Ahmed bellowed.

Ridan, hearing Ahmed, rushed to the edge of the ship, and grabbed the rope, but he was not strong enough to pull them aboard. "Keep holding the rope!" Ahmed yelled. "There's a ladder at the other side of the ship. Swim!" Ahmed said, and they both swam to the other side, where they found the ladder.

They collapsed on the deck. They were alive! "Thanks," Ahmed said, "Although, that was a rash decision." Safra smiled. Ridan joined them.

"Let's help the Captain out of the hold," he said. "Yeah, let's go!" Safra said. Ridan quickly steered the ship around.

Because the ship was headed around the island, the wind had become a gentle breeze. They climbed into the hold, where they found the Captain, upside down, in a barrel.

"Oh, Captain, how did you get yourself in this one?" Safra sighed.

Ahmed lifted him out. "Oh, I feel dizzy," the Captain said, and shook his head. "You two look like you fell into the ocean! What happened?" he asked.

"Captain, you need some rest. Relax," Ahmed said. They took him into a cabin, and Ridan was put in charge of steering the ship. All of the sailors were still asleep. "I don't know how these guys slept through this," Ahmed said. "Years of experience, I guess."

"Yeah," Safra chuckled.

"We're so close to the island!" Ridan exclaimed.

It was amazing, but it did not look like a normal island. Snow-covered landscape, frozen lakes— it felt like they were in another world.

I closed my eyes —again. I was in a bright meadow near a forest. I turned around to see a white fox. It whimpered, as if to tell me something.

It kept staring at me, and everything melted away into black again. Safra shook her head. No one had noticed her drifting off. They seemed even closer to the island, and she stared at a large peak, and her sharp eyes could see a black figure walk across the snow.

"Ridan, look at that!" she pointed.

It had disappeared.

"What?" he asked.

"Nothing…I thought I saw something…I saw a black creature," she shrugged.

"Maybe it was a shadow," he said, not paying much attention to what she was saying.

"Yeah…you're right," she said.

But she could have sworn she had seen something else.

NINE

SILVER ISLAND

They soon reached the back of the island. Everyone was up and about, taking out supplies, weaving more rope, and brushing up the rowboats. "Attention everyone," the Captain said. "I have an announcement. Ever since Safra and Ridan encountered a dangerous creature, we now know that we will face such obstacles, maybe even worse. And to solve that problem, we will split into groups of five. The first group will go through the island and draw maps, and they should be back before dark. Then, the next day we will send the second group. Got it? We will select the first team when we dock on the island," he said. "Back to work, everybody!"

The thought of the plaque came back to Safra. She had to find a way to join in the first group because she desperately wanted to know about the consequences it had mentioned. She would have to take care of that later, though. It was a time to be proud of what she had done. *I have succeeded in finding Silver Island, at last,* she thought. *I did it! I did it,* she smiled.

"We did it! We found Silver Island!" she yelled to Ridan.
"Yeah. But don't keep your hopes up," he said.
"What!? I don't even care that much about the magic sand! I told you, we found it! That's all I care about, for now," she said, and clenched her fists.

He's so pessimistic sometimes, she thought. *Why did he say that? He's probably in a bad mood.*

About half an hour later, the ship had docked at a suitable place. Instead of celebrating, they started unloading supplies. "It seems as if they think yesterday's partying is enough," Safra chuckled.

She heard a loud laugh from behind, and she turned to see Ahmed. "Yes, yes! Get to work, Safra!" He smiled, and went back to work.

She stood there, staring at the beautiful scene and everything looked like what she had seen in her first vision, but one thing looked out of place. She had expected to be different types of animals. But even in her vision, she had not seen any signs of life.

"That's puzzling," she wondered aloud.

"Everyone, listen to me! Let's set up camp!" the Captain said.

They worked for hours, and finally decided to set up the camp suitable for the men from the main ship, and everyone else would stay on the other ships. Safra was glad that she could stay on the island—a perfect way to gain an excuse to explore.

"Attention, attention! I, the Captain, have some rules—because some of us are staying on the island," he said. Everyone groaned. "First of all, there will be no exploring until I say that we can. This is for your own safety. You can only explore when you are part of a group. Second, always stick with at least one of your fellow crew members, and try to stay together as a group. Third, all of you will obey these rules and my orders. You will not disobey, understood?"

He sounded somewhat harsh to Safra, and she was disappointed that she could not explore. *Well, I'll join a group soon, so I don't have to worry,* she thought. Ridan looked annoyed.

"He just seems so harsh and cold," she muttered. "Let's just hope we'll get in a group first."

"Which we will! We discovered Silver Island! The Captain will definitely let us be in the first group," Ridan said. "If he doesn't I'll—I'll—I don't know what I will do," he said and laughed.

Safra laughed too, and she now had more confidence. What could she lose?

"I'm going to choose the groups now! Everyone, settle down," said the Captain, standing on a tree stump. All the sailors gathered around him, eagerly waiting.

"Ok," he said, taking out a piece of paper, "The first group will consist of…Let's see…Ben, William, Mark, Leon, and…Tom. You all have the honor of being the first group!" he exclaimed, "I will go in the second one," he continued.

Safra was shocked. "Captain…I want to go," she said.

"No, no, you and Ridan are important," he murmured.

"That coward! He wants others to go and see how dangerous it will be. That's why he wants to go in the second group, including us!" Ridan clenched his teeth. Safra had no words.Of course. He had been suspicious…

But I still wanted to go in the first one.

She sighed and dragged her feet against the snow. It was so cold; everyone had to wear fluffy, huge coats made of sheep wool. Even though it kept her warm, Safra hated it. It made her feel like she was squished into a heated box, imprisoned. She liked to be free.

You are getting in the first group, she promised herself. It made her feel better, even though she was feeling quite miserable in this island. There was no life, no freedom, and rules. These were all things she hated.

She stared at Ridan standing near the snowy shore, which now had a small amount of normal sand. He was studying the small specimens of fish, noting them down.

She sighed. When were they going to do some real exploring? She stared longingly at the large volcano in the far distance. She felt like she had a mini-war going on inside her mind, one side telling her to break the rules, the other to wait for her turn.

"Safra! Let's go! Dinner!" Ridan's call broke her moment of thought.

"Coming!" she shouted. She padded to the main tent through the snow, still thinking about her problems.

"Maybe a good, tasty dinner will help," she said to herself.

TEN

DINNER

When Safra reached the main tent, dinner had already started. Ridan waved, beckoning her to come and sit with him. She also noticed that Chuck and Ahmed were there as well.

She sat next to them, and Chuck said, "Safra! How do you feel about being on Silver Island?"

"Great! Thank you for all your help! I really owe you one," she said.

"Lucky chaps who got into the first group," Ahmed said, obviously not happy with the Captain. He slouched in his chair, frowning.

"Lucky? Seriously," Safra muttered.

"Safra, is something wrong?" Ridan asked quietly. "I wanted to be in the first group too," she sighed. "Look, maybe we'll be in the same group as the Captain! That will be fun…Right?" Chuck said, unsure of Safra's reaction.

"Yeah, sure it'll be fun," she rolled her eyes.

"It won't be that bad," Ridan said.

Safra grumbled. Why was everything going wrong for her?

"Hey," Ahmed said, "If it'll make you feel better, here you go." He handed Safra a small leather notebook with beautiful golden embroidery, and an antique fountain pen. "You can use it to write down stuff about your adventures. I picked it up in Baghdad," he said proudly.

"Thanks Ahmed, but I won't be having adventures very soon," she said, wondering how he could just give away something so easily.

"Keep it. Don't be silly. You'll probably be in the second group." he said.

Safra picked at her food. She didn't feel like eating at all.

"Shake it off, Safra," she whispered to herself.

She managed to gobble it down, and went outside of the tent and opened the notebook. She gripped the pen in her hand, and began to write:

June 9th, 8:45 pm.

It's cold outside. I can't stop thinking about exploring, and the Captain is being such a coward, and I hate it. Ooh, HOW I HATE IT! He's acting so brave, and he doesn't deserve to be the Captain. Ahmed does. He cares about the ship, fellow shipmates, and Ridan and me as well. Chuck, Ahmed and Ridan were trying to make me feel better, because I was in a bad mood because the Captain wouldn't let me be in the first group. I wanted to find out more about Meera and those consequences that paper mentioned. Those men who were selected don't know anything about this, and they may be in danger.

Safra

She had decided to call it *Safra's Log*. She was happy that Ahmed had given it to her.

Safra smiled. Maybe it wasn't so bad after all. She had to remain optimistic if she wanted to feel good.

She took a deep breath and stared out at the calm sea.

ELEVEN

THE FIRST GROUP DEPARTS

Safra's Log
June 10th, 7:04 am

The first group is getting ready for their adventure. They have packed rucksacks filled with food, water, compasses, papers and pencils to draw out maps, and extra clothes. Oh, how I envy them! But still, I can go next time. And maybe, Chuck and Ahmed would come along in my group! That would be so fun! That's better than going along with these weirdos who I don't know at all.

But I still have a battle going on in my head. I want to break the rules and explore, but then, I don't want to. It could ruin my chance of being in a group, and I would probably get caught. Well, I guess that clears it.

Safra

Safra closed her notebook and glanced at the first group.
They were in danger, and she could do nothing about it.
Maybe I'll talk to the Captain, she thought, and walked up to
him.

"Captain… Since my brother and I led you to Silver
Island, could we be in the first group?" she pleaded. She
knew that it probably would not work.

"No, my dear…Not now," he said.

"Why aren't you going in the first group?" she asked.
"Because…I wanted some of them to have the honor,"
he stammered.

"Then why didn't you send Ahmed along with them?
He's your right -hand man," she said, narrowing her eyes.
"Um…Well, I always let him do the honors," he said,
sweat trickling down his forehead.

"Yeah, so why not this time?" she grilled.

"Because…I don't know! You ask too many questions! I
don't have time for this!" he looked exasperated.

"I know the real reason," Safra muttered and walked
away. "Time for a day full of waiting and boredom." She
dreaded the fact that she could get in trouble for not
mentioning the plaque. The Captain was not to be
trusted, and who else could she confide in? Not Ahmed
or Chuck, they wouldn't believe her. Ridan didn't believe
it already. What could she do?
I can't do anything, I'm helpless, she thought sadly.
Something could happen to them.
But she realized that maybe the men would be smart,
and follow the rules. Maybe they would come back safely.
I'm worrying too much. I should calm down.
She watched them walk into the bleak, white wilderness,
proud that they had been picked first. But in one way or
another, Safra was happy. If they made some valuable
discoveries, it could be easier than she thought. She

would make sure to read the maps that they would draw out. *I'll be serious about this,* she thought.

She felt better after giving that small pep talk to herself. She walked out of her tent and the cool air seemed to embrace her. She didn't bother to wear her coat, and she allowed the ice -cold water to sweep over her feet. It was peculiar to feel the seawater without the hot sand or the sun. She sighed, staring at the empty gray sky.

I closed my eyes once more, only I am now in a forest. It looks bizarre without any leaves. The sky darkens. I blink, and a thick wall of branches curls behind me. I try to push and break it, but it is too strong! I realize that there is no other way out. I am imprisoned!

Safra blinked. What could this vision mean? She could not understand.

Bewildered, she decided to find the others. She started running to the main tent, where she found Ridan, Chuck, and Ahmed sitting and chatting.

They greeted her warmly. "I got another vision," she hissed at Ridan. "What?" he said out loud.

She sighed. "You can tell them," Ridan said reassuringly.

She started to explain that she had visions, ever since her locket had somehow activated.

"Safra, you didn't fool us. I know you and Ridan cooked that up!" Ahmed laughed.

"If you are standing in a magical island that has snow in summer, and is supposed to hold magical sand, you can believe this," she said, slowly starting to get angry.

"Ahmed…Maybe…Think about it. How did they steer the boat towards Polaris, then? Safra, you might be right." Chuck jumped up and down.

Ahmed looked shocked and reluctant. "Wow. I think that this is a wonderful advantage," he said, and grinned.

"Okay, I need your opinions on this. I just had a vision that I'm in a forest, and suddenly the tree branches curl into a thick wall behind me, and I can't escape. What do you think that means?" she asked.

"It means that you are going to be in a forest, and there's going to be a wall of branches behind you, and you can't escape," Chuck said.

"Chuck! Not like that! I don't understand why I was alone. If I was in a group, there are supposed to be other people, right? What if I broke the rules or something? I'm scared," Safra admitted.

"Don't worry. Just keep in the urge to break the rules. Keep calm," Ahmed said.

"But wait. All the visions I had so far have come true."

"Calm down," Ridan said, sighing. "Yeah, I'll do that." She nodded.

"Hey dudes, the Captain said that he's going to be selecting the second group!" Jon, the deckhand, said. They scrambled outside, to the tree stump, where the Captain was standing.

"Everyone, I am hereby choosing the second group! It shall consist of Ahmed, Safra, Ridan, Jorge, and me as well."

"Aww...Chuck, maybe next time," Safra rubbed his shoulder.

"I wasn't made for anything anyway. Jorge, the scaredy-cat gets picked instead of me," Chuck said, and walked away. "Now I know why I'm just a janitor." He walked into his tent, hands clenched into fists.

"Chuck!" Ahmed yelled, but he did not answer.

Jorge seemed to shiver in fear, but sneered at Chuck confidently, which bothered Safra. She grumbled in irritation. "I'll take care of you later."

TWELVE

NIGHTFALL

Night fell, and the first group had not returned.

"Poor Chuck," Ridan said.

"He hasn't come out of his tent ever since," Ahmed said.

"Should we try and cheer him up?" Safra suggested.

"I don't know."

The Captain called everyone to the tree stump again for a meeting. "As you can see, the first group has not arrived, and there is no sign from them. Let's go and get them! Is everyone with me?" he pumped his fist in the air.

Then, a puny voice crushed the silence.

"Captain, I would like to be excused from this adventure," Jorge said. He was trying hard to look brave.

"We have a coward in our hands. Would anybody else like to volunteer?" The Captain did not seem to care at all. Jorge turned red and shrunk to the back of the crowd.

But, only one pudgy hand rose up.

"Who is that? I cannot see you!" he demanded. All the other sailors turned their heads towards Chuck. "I want to join, sir. I really want to."

Everyone started to laugh. "Chuck? Chuck? Are you kidding me?" Jorge laughed nervously.

"Silence! He was our only volunteer! We should take him!" Ahmed pushed the Captain off the stump and took his place. "Stop laughing!" He bellowed.

Everyone was surprised because of Ahmed's outburst, and by this time the Captain had gotten up. He glared at Ahmed, who slowly stepped down and returned to his place with Safra and Ridan.

"Yes, Ahmed. I intend to take him. That was not necessary," the Captain said, still glaring.

Safra congratulated Chuck, and gave him a pat on the back.

"Thank you," he said, looking quite proud.

He flashed a superior smile at Jorge, who in turn scowled and muttered something under his breath.

"Now, what do you think happened to those men?" Ahmed said, once they were inside Safra's tent.

Safra had not thought about that one bit! It was all her fault. What had she done? *I should have told someone anyway,* she thought. Five men had just disappeared, just like that. She raced to the others and blurted out the whole story about Meera and the plaque.

"Yes…Very interesting, indeed," Chuck said.

Safra's head was filled with all the possibilities. Could they have been trapped? Were they just late? Or…Something worse…Could they have been killed? There was no trace of them, and that was what she worried most about. Now they didn't even have maps!

"Oh…Why does it have to be like this?" she groaned. "What if we fail?"

"Stop talking about failing!" Ridan groaned.

"Well, I guess it's up to us to bring them back. I mean us four. The Captain isn't going to do anything," Ridan said.
"Um…Excuse me?" Ahmed raised an eyebrow.
"Can't you see it? He sent other people he didn't care about before he went, just to test it out! He didn't send you, his right hand man, because you are important to him. He didn't want anything to happen to you," Safra said.
Ahmed realized the truth. "That chicken," he said, and slumped into his seat.
"That's not something to think about now, Ahmed. Past is past. We need to think of a plan for tomorrow, and we need to pack," Safra said, "Let's go get some bags or something."
Chuck and Ridan went to the main tent to gather some supplies, and Safra soon came back with some satchels and rucksacks.
They spent the night placing ample amounts of sandwiches, fruits, paper, pencils, compasses, torches, machetes, water canteens, weapons such as bows and arrows, daggers, and knives, water filters, toothbrushes, and other necessities.
They were done. They sat next to the fire, for a well-earned rest. Safra stomach growled ferociously. Luckily, a fruit basket lay within her reach. She picked up an orange, and began peeling it.
"Be careful," Ahmed said.
"Careful with what?" she asked.
"The orange. Orange peels catch fire, you know." He smiled. "It's something very peculiar. We don't expect some things, and they happen. Sometimes, we expect some things to happen, but they don't."

Turning to the others, he said, "Okay, that's done. Now let's think of a plan."

That was weird, she thought.

"Okay, let's just keep some rules. Stay together, and never chicken out," Chuck said. "That's it."

"Yeah! We don't need any plans! Who knows what we will face?" Ridan said.

"I, Ahmed, solemnly pledge that I will follow our rules."

"I, Safra…"

"I, Ridan…"

"I, Chuck…"

THIRTEEN

THE ADVENTURE BEGINS

The morning light flooded through Ridan's tent as he awoke. He rubbed his eyes, and realized that today was the day. Today was the day they would begin their adventure!

He threw back his blanket, and ran to the main tent, where he saw Safra, Chuck, and Ahmed sitting at the table, eating jam rolls for breakfast.

"Ridan! There you are!" Ahmed said.

"You didn't even comb your hair!" Safra chuckled.

"Ugh. I guess I forgot. I was too sleepy," he said as he sat down.

"Eww. Yuck! You didn't brush your teeth either, did you?" Safra laughed.

Chuck wrinkled his nose.

"I rushed," Ridan admitted.

"Then I don't think you want some of these jam rolls," Ahmed taunted.

Ridan grunted and went to the ship to brush his teeth.
They shared a good laugh, and ate heartily. They would
need their energy for today.
Safra walked out on the shore while Ridan went to eat,
and took out her notebook and began to write:

Safra's Log

June 11th, 7:35 am
The first group did not return yesterday, so the second
group is supposed to find them. Captain, Ahmed, Chuck,
Ridan and I are in the group! Today our adventure starts,
and I cannot wait. But I am worried that it is kind of my
fault that they disappeared. I should have told someone.
Maybe I should have told Ridan, Chuck or Ahmed. Oh,
now I have to find them, or I'll be guilty for the rest of my
life!

I had a weird vision just the other day, about a forest. I
hope it doesn't come true.

Safra

She closed the book and stuffed it in her bag. She stared
out at the dull gray and white landscape.
She watched Chuck, Ahmed, and Ridan bringing their
rucksacks. The time had come.
"Ready to go, everyone?" Ahmed asked.
"Yes, of course! But where's the Captain?" she said.

"I'll go check," Chuck said, and he lifted the flap of the tent to see the Captain packing his rucksack at the last minute.

"Chuck! Just in time! Help me pack this, will you?" he asked sheepishly, stuffing things into it.

"Captain! We're leaving now! Quickly!" Ahmed yelled. They managed to get the Captain ready, and he insisted that he would give one final speech to everyone.

"I give my final orders before we leave for the depths of Silver Island. If I do not return, do not send any other groups. Do not panic. It may take us days, weeks, months, years. I take leave of you all. I will bring the men back, and you all must stay safe. At the first sight of danger, you must leave this place."

At that moment, Safra sensed a genuine part of the Captain coming to life. He was not his arrogant, cowardly self, he had been truthful. He wanted to protect his fellow sailors. She could even see tears welling up in his eyes, and she knew he was scared. All of them were scared, but excited and honored that they just might be the heroes of tomorrow. *It's time for me to prove myself to the world,* Safra thought. *No, it's time for us to prove ourselves to the world. There's no 'I' in this team.*

She decided to keep that as something to remember. "I won't forget it," she whispered to herself. "Safra! We are leaving!" Ridan yelled out.

She rushed to join them. They headed out towards the forest, which lay miles ahead.

Ridan said, "Is this really happening?"

"Of course, buddy, it's happening." Ahmed smiled a toothy smile, and thumped Ridan on the back.

All of them smiled, even the Captain let out a hearty laugh. Safra guessed that he needed something to get his mind off the whole adventure that lay ahead.

All of them seemed to be a little nervous. *Of course, everyone would be nervous,* she thought.

 But for Safra, only one thing remained in her mind. The adventure had begun.

FOURTEEN

THE FIRST OBSTACLE

They soon reached a large meadow that lay before the forest. The long grass and flowers were a surprise. There was no snow, and the sun's warmth felt like rain after a drought.

"Do you get this? The season changed. It's like spring!" Chuck exclaimed, He got down on his belly and rolled around in the flowers. Safra decided to follow suit.

"The smell of the flowers…It makes me feel weird, like I want to pick them." Safra sniffed, "Oh, and look at that!" She pointed at a flower bud that popped open, and sparkly, golden, glowing pieces of pollen rained out.

"Stop being so childish, all of you! We have to get going!" The Captain said, and started walking fast. "Slow down!" Ahmed yelled, and they had to run to catch up to the Captain.

But Safra kept looking at the flowers. The urge to pick them became stronger.

"Wait." The Captain stopped in his tracks. "These flowers…Are so pretty…" He kneeled down next to one.

"Wait, the flower's scent… It's controlling us…"Ahmed
warned, but he felt himself trying to grab a flower.

All of them grabbed one, separating it from the ground.
Safra felt a large gust of wind circling her, filled with the
same scent of the mysterious flower. She blinked, and the
wind stopped. She was suddenly hit by a cold draft, and
large snowflakes covered her face. She was stuck in a
blizzard! "Ridan! Chuck! Ahmed! Captain? Anybody!" she
shouted until her voice was hoarse.

She collapsed on the cold, hard ground, hopeless.
She was sure that she was going to be lost forever, in the
cold, left to starve. Her whole body felt numb, and she
could only feel the crushed flower in her hand.

*I closed my eyes, once more, like I always did when I got a vision.
This time I could see a crackling fire, underneath a golden
mantelpiece shaped like a peacock. There was Meera's face in the
fire, and a hand threw a sparkling powder in it. Then everything
faded away.*

Safra slowly opened her eyes. She was covered in a
warm, thick blanket, and she was lying down on a couch.
She noticed that she was in a cabin of some sort. A fire
crackled next to her feet, under the same mantelpiece.
The door creaked open, and a lady entered the room.
"You have awakened, it seems," she said in a voice that
almost sounded like a whisper. She wore gray and white
robes with thick and colorful beads hanging around her
neck. Bright red lipstick accentuated her beautiful face.
Her jet-black hair was slicked back into a bun, and her
soft, emerald eyes met Safra's bold, chocolate ones.

"I found you in the cold. What are you, a young girl,
doing here?"

"I am part of the crew. On The Ships," she said,
suspecting that the lady might not even know what The
Ships were.

"Oh, yes. They have found it this year, haven't they?"
She smiled mysteriously.

"How…" Safra stammered.

"I know."

"But…"

"I just know."

"But how do you know?"

"If you are a part of the Ships, doesn't that mean they
are here?" She laughed good-heartedly.

"Who are you?" Safra asked, ignoring her joke.

"My name is Zelda." she smiled.

Safra stared at the fire, and Meera appeared, just like her
vision. Then Zelda grabbed a powder and tossed it into
the flames, causing it to burn out.

"You can see her, can't you?" Zelda looked at her
questioningly.

"Yes, I can." Safra said, bewildered.

"You do not understand," she said, "that, if you can see
things like that, you are special."

"I get *visions*."

"You are a Seer, and you can defeat her. You may be one
of the last Seers the world will have. And you can do it."

"Defeat who?"

Zelda whispered. "The locket does not hold the power
now. You hold the power. Take this, and plant a flower.
After you wish for it to take you somewhere, an identical
flower will be planted at your destination, and once you
pick it, you will be transported there. But remember, it
cannot be used for everything you desire, and it only

grows in snow." Zelda said, and she vanished, along with the house.

Safra was outside, but the blizzard had stopped. She had also been wrapped with a fur coat. She studied the pouch, and she could see faded lettering on the cloth. It read: *Azella Seeds*.

"Azella? Is that what these flowers are called?" She murmured.

Safra got to work. She dug a hole in the ground, and placed a seed inside. From the moisture from the snow, it immediately started to grow. The bud burst open, and it was just like the ones in the meadow.

"Take me to Ridan, Chuck, Ahmed, and the Captain," she whispered, and picked the flower. A gust of wind circled her once more.

FIFTEEN

TOGETHER AGAIN

She found herself in the end of the warm, sunny meadow, with the Captain, Ahmed, Chuck and Ridan by her side.

"Oh! I was so scared that we would never find each other again!" Ridan hugged Safra.

"It's okay now," Safra whispered into his ear.

"I was trapped in a dark attic with a lot of bugs," Chuck shuddered as he told his story.

"I was chased by a tiger in a desert," Ahmed said.

"I was stuck in a quicksand pit in a rainforest," the Captain looked terrified.

"And I was stuck in a house, with spirits and ghosts," Ridan said. "Suddenly a gust of wind circled me, and I came here."

Safra told them about her experience with the woman, but excluded the Seer part. She would tell Ridan, Ahmed, and Chuck, but not the Captain. When he walked ahead, she told the rest to them about it. "What?" Chuck looked blown away.

"Azella? It can help us travel to the volcano!" Ahmed exclaimed. "Azella was the flower that separated us!"
"She said it wouldn't work for all our desires," she said.
"But this is important!" Ridan argued.
"No. This is a desire for us to find the sand, right?"
"No! We need to rescue the men," he said.
"I don't know. I don't think it will work, because she also said it only grows in snow, and that could be a problem," Safra said.
"Ridan, Safra's right, I guess. We should find out more about these so called Azella seeds," Ahmed said.
"Let's just make sure to stay together this time, okay?" Chuck said.
"Yeah…We will." Safra smiled at him.
As they walked through the meadow, they stopped for water and fruits.
"Ridan! Look at that!" Safra pointed to a beautiful white fox standing by a tree, her watchful eyes scrutinizing them from head to toe.
She whimpered, just like in her vision. "Try to talk to her!" she said.
"That's the problem. I can't," he said, "No matter how hard I try!"
"How could that be?" she looked at him, concerned. "Are you feeling okay?"
"Yeah. There's no problem with me!"
"Just making sure."
What is this fox trying to tell me? Hmmm, she thought. *I will find out later. But right now, I feel so tired.*
Everyone was exhausted, especially the Captain.
"Can we even do this?" he panted.
"What do you mean, Captain?" Ahmed look astonished.

"I mean, this flower thing left us in this state. How are we going to go on and on? Why can't we just go back while we can?" the Captain sighed.

He looked so down in the dumps that Safra felt sorry for him.

"No, no Captain, you're just tired. That's why you're thinking things like this. Just take some rest," Chuck reassured him.

"No. I can't do this," he said.

"Come on, Captain! We have to keep going! This is your dream! No, this is *our* dream! We can't give up now! We have to always stay motivated. We cannot lose hope with ourselves. We can do this. I know we can," Safra sat down next him.

"Ok. Fine," he said, but he still did not look certain. "We shall go on."

"That's the spirit, Captain!" Ridan smiled.

They decided to start their next part of their journey: through the forest. Safra wondered if this was the forest from her vision, and if it was, she was not sure if she wanted to experience it. She had been shook by the vision, and she did not know how she would feel in real life. But, she knew she had to face it.

Safra looked around. She knew that all of them were a little disheveled from the flower incident, but all of them except the Captain seemed really good at hiding it. They all looked and acted brave. Maybe she and the Captain were scared, and others weren't.

I hope that's not true.

SIXTEEN

FEAR

It seemed like they had been walking forever. The distance looked short, but it really wasn't. They still had a long way to go, but they did not stop. The journey also was very silent as nobody spoke. All of them seemed to be in their own world, daydreaming about what lay before them.

They finally stood before the forest. A large, wooden sign stood in their way, like a scarecrow watching over a cornfield.

"Hmmm…It says…"

**Fear may be something that everyone does hate,
But if you do not face it soon, it will be too late.
Beware of this place,
 IF the thought of your fear makes your heart pace.
And in the end if you fail,
You will fall into a dark jail,
The only way to be saved is by a friend,
who will be with you until the end.**

"I think I get it," Ridan said. "This is supposed to be facing your fears?"

"Yeah…Although I don't know what my fear is, anyway. I'm scared of a lot of things," Safra said. "Me too," Chuck nodded.

"I guess me too," the Captain said.

Ahmed looked at the board with a smile. "This will be easy," he said and walked past the sign with an air of confidence to his stride.

They entered the eerie forest, and Safra noticed that she had the same feeling as in her vision, about the leaves on the trees. This was not a good start.

Suddenly the whole sky darkened. The rest of them had disappeared! She was all alone. An uneasy feeling overcame her. She had failed. "I'm a failure. I'm a failure," Safra choked out. She had lost them. She had lost herself, in this cold, dark world.

The thick wall of branches curled themselves over the entrance. *I can't go back. I'm going to stay here and cry for the rest of my life,* she thought.

Wait. There is no I in a team, remember? I have to try and go on. What about our rules? We have to stay together!

Safra stood up. She knew there was nothing to be scared of. She had to go on. Then she realized that she was facing her fear.

Ridan stared at the dull landscape. Where was everyone? "Probably facing fears," he thought aloud.

The sky turned to a murky black.

Suddenly, his brain seemed crammed with thoughts of his parents, his problems. But he was not like himself. He could not think of any solutions. Nothing. Nothing at all. It seemed to overwhelm him; Safra's visions, the time when his power didn't work, his parents, his grandpa, the silver sand, the Captain, Chuck, Safra, Ahmed, this forest, what was the next obstacle— all of his problems seemed to crowd his head at the same time.

He felt like cracking from the pressure, but he also knew that this was his fear. "I have to overcome it. I have to," he said and kept walking.

All of his problems seemed to come alive before his very eyes. The sides of the path had misty visions of his thoughts. It was like he could see what was going on in his mind! Even if he kept his head down, he could hear them. They did not stop.

"If I have to face them, I will," he said, and turned to look at the mist, and as he looked at it directly, they vanished.

"Wait…"

He looked at the visions directly again, and they vanished again, one by one.

The sky turned into a bright blue, and Ridan could see Safra standing a few feet away.

"Safra!"

"Ridan!"

"You're here!"

"Funny. You appeared right after I conquered my fear." Safra said. "Same for me," he replied.

Chuck and the Captain appeared next. "Yes! I conquered mine easily!" Chuck exclaimed. He was so happy he lifted both Ridan and Safra off the ground.

"It wasn't so bad, actually," the Captain said. "I felt bad, at first, because it appears that my fear is being laughed at. Humph," he said, and frowned. "Mine is being lonely," Chuck said.

"We know." Safra laughed.

"And that would have been easy to conquer," Ridan said. "But where is Ahmed? He should be here by now," the Captain said, scratching his head.

"Wait. What if he didn't conquer his fear?" Ridan stared at Safra, and gave her a look that meant: *We've got to do something about this.*

Safra understood. "We have to find him," she said. Well, we aren't too far away from the camp. One of us could go and call for help, and get more men," the Captain suggested.

"No…When I was facing my fear, a thick wall of branches blocked the entrance. We can't go back," Safra said.

"What do we do now?" Chuck started chewing on his fingernails.

Safra gritted her teeth.

"I don't know. We have to think of the solution, and fast."

SEVENTEEN

AHMED

Ahmed got ready to face his fear. "I have nothing to be afraid of," he scoffed proudly.

 A thick, white mist wafted through the path. Ahmed could not see anything, and suddenly, a shape formed. First a blob, then a person, then the Captain, Safra, Ridan, and Chuck formed. All of them were leaving him. They were waving to him, saying things like, "Bye Ahmed, we're going to find the silver sand and get rich. We don't need you. You are going to stay here forever." Betrayal. Distrust. His worst fear.

Ahmed knew this was the time to face his fear, but he could not bear it. He could not subdue the pressure. Then suddenly, the whole ground cracked open under Ahmed's feet, creating a deep gorge beneath him.

 But, as he began to plummet downwards, his shirt caught onto a branch.

"Phew," he sighed. "That was a miracle."

No surprise, but even that betrayed him. 'RIP' went his shirt.

He fell. Down, down, down, into the deep darkness, waiting for the end…

Safra sat down on a rock, thinking about the possible things that could have happened to Ahmed.

"Guys…come and look at this!" Chuck pointed at a large gorge.

"It wasn't there a few minutes ago!" Ridan exclaimed, and went closer to examine it.

"And look at that! That branch, over there, has a piece of cloth stuck to it. It's Ahmed's!" the Captain pointed.

"Does that mean…Do we go in?" she asked.

Safra heard a rustling in the bushes. She turned to see the white fox standing there.

Yes, you must go after your friend, it's safe, she seemed to say.

"Are you kidding me? We'll die!" Ridan exclaimed. Safra took a deep breath and untied her shoes. She took one last look at the rest of them, and jumped into the gorge.

"Safra? Are you crazy?"

Their voices faded away. She knew that it was now too late to try and save herself.

It's like the gorge never ends, she thought.

Then, the cool feeling of water hit her body. She tried to swim up to the surface, but it was impossible. With each stroke, she felt like she was being pulled deeper. Surprisingly, she could easily open her eyes. She could see sparkling coral and beautiful seals chasing each other. But now she was stuck there as well, and she could not hold her breath in much longer. "Uh," she grunted. She felt an uncomfortable tightening in her throat. Her lungs felt like they would burst, and she felt like she was being deflated, deprived of air.

She squinted through her closing eyes, trying as hard as possible to swim upward.

A peculiar feeling washed over Safra. Her legs came close to each other, fusing together. A bright light illuminated the water, turning it into a bright blue color. Her feet pointed outwards, and shaped themselves into a tail. More skin grew over her legs speckled with a glossy grey sheen. It was a seal tail!

Wait. Somehow I'm holding my breath. It's so easy! I could hold it for an hour at this point, she thought.

Oh, yeah, now I'm half human and half seal. I need to find Ahmed!

She heard a huge splash from overhead. She looked up at the water's surface, where the Captain, Chuck, and Ridan had jumped in. She watched their legs turn into seal tails as well. "Safra! I was so worried!" Ridan swam towards her. They could easily communicate too!

"No time. We need to find Ahmed," Safra said. She spotted a dark cave on her left. She stared at it. *How come I didn't notice this before?*

"This way," she said and swam towards the cave.

Safra soon became accustomed to her tail. It allowed her to push forward with strong strokes and swim longer without getting tired.

As they entered the cave's mouth, Safra sensed a strong current. "Ahmed must have been dragged down here," she said.

"Do you think he was turned into a seal, too?" the Captain asked.

"Wait. Maybe if we went inside, we could come back because we are half seals. Maybe because Ahmed didn't face his fear, he didn't turn into a half seal. I think we could bear this current," she said, and put out her hand to test it. "Let the current take you down," she said, and went limp. It carried her to the cave, where it sloped downwards. She fell down a long way onto the hard, cold, ground, but she was not hurt. Her tail changed back to her own legs, as there was no water.

The others followed suit. "Wow. I wonder why the water doesn't flood this place," Chuck murmured.

"Mm…" Safra nodded absentmindedly.

She walked deeper into the cave, disappearing into the darkness. She hoped that she would find Ahmed, and they could escape safely.

EIGHTEEN

THE GIRL

Safra walked through the cave, staring at carved drawings. Pictures of a beautiful castle, a garden, and horses were etched in the walls, preserved forever.
An elegant portrait of Meera caught her eye. *Who is she? And who drew her? And why is she appearing everywhere?*
Safra's hand brushed the walls, exploring every story that lay deep inside the drawings.
She stopped walking, and she seemed to hear something. "Who are you? Go away!" Someone shouted. Voices drifted through the air.
Her legs automatically started running towards the sounds. *Pit-pat-pit-pat-pit-pat-pit-pat* went her bare feet. The sounds became louder, and she turned left into a room, carved in the hard rock.
"Ahmed!" she shouted, and ran towards him.
Why does he look irritated?
She turned her head to see a girl, about her own age, standing in the corner. Her once shiny, brunette hair now was filled with tangles and mud. Her pale face had a tone

of sadness to it, and she looked very familiar. Her sharp, hazel eyes stared right through Safra like an arrow. "Now there's another one! Why are you here?" she groaned.

Safra frowned at the girl's sassy attitude. "Well, I'm here to take my friend," she said back.

"Who are you anyway?" the girl said, ignoring her answer. "I am Safra, and these are my friends," Safra said calmly. "Who are you?"

She started laughing hysterically. "You don't know who I am? Really? Don't lie," she said and laid a hand on Safra's shoulder.

"No, I actually don't," she replied, narrowing her eyes. "I am Raisha. You could almost call me a ruler!" Her eyes gleamed with pride and authority.

"Well. How come a *ruler* like you is sitting down here, in an abandoned cave?" Ahmed rolled his eyes.

"I was caught, imprisoned, and left down here forever," she flicked her head upwards, as if remembering something that had happened a long time ago.

"You did these drawings?" Safra asked.

"Why, yes, of course," Raisha said.

"Then how do you know her?" she pointed to the portrait of Meera. Raisha hung her head, and remained silent. "Are you here only for your friend?" she asked coldly, ignoring Safra once more.

"Umm… Safra longed to ask her why she was imprisoned, but she was afraid that it would hurt her feelings again.

Raisha seemed to read her mind. "I was on a quest. It was made sure that I could not face my fear," she said solemnly.

"Who made sure…?" Ridan trailed off.

Raisha did not answer.

"How about you come with us," the Captain said. "We will free you, and you can continue with your quest," he suggested.

She mumbled something under her breath.

"I'll take that as a yes," he said.

Ahmed's jaw seemed to drop to the floor. He clearly did not like Raisha, and was not expecting them to take her along.

"Come on, let's go," Safra said. She did not take a second look at Raisha, but she knew she was somewhat involved in their quest as well. She knew that were some secrets that would just have to be revealed later.

They easily climbed up the slope, using the smooth stones as steps. "Ahmed, what exactly happened to you when you fell down here?" Safra asked.

"I fell into the water, and then I was sucked into the cave, where I was stuck with that *psycho*," he whispered the last word.

Safra nodded. She didn't want to disagree with Ahmed, but she didn't want to insult the girl either. Safra thought that she was interesting. *She knows Meera, and she has a mysterious quest of her own that she won't reveal. Hmmm…*
Soon, the stone steps came to an end. A steep cliff peered down at them, covered in spiky rocks.

"It seems easy to climb. Those rocks seem sturdy. We can use those as footholds," Ridan observed.

Raisha shook her head. "It's impossible. I've tried before."

"But you didn't face your fear. Obviously it wouldn't have worked for you," he said, smiling proudly.

"But it might not be easy as you think. It's hard…"

"You can't argue with flawless logic," he answered. Raisha opened her mouth to say something. "Both of you, stop bickering." Chuck sighed. "We need to start climbing."

Safra placed a foot on the first rock and took a deep breath. *Climb,* she told herself, as she went higher and higher. *It's like you are back in Erina, climbing cliffs.* Her mind was suddenly filled with the thoughts of home. Homesickness finally seemed to overwhelm her, even though she had lasted this long without thinking of it. *Grandpa.*

Suddenly, she felt like she could not move a muscle. She snapped out of her reverie, finally making note of how high she was. Her grip on the rocks loosened, and she toppled over the edge.

Falling did not scare her. Safra felt like she was held in a trance, like she could close her eyes forever.

I close my eyes. I see a beautiful girl with shining, curly brown hair standing on a balcony of a large palace, dressed in a beautiful lace gown with a matching veil. People stand before her, throwing flowers. She waves to everyone, her gold jewelry tinkling with a beautiful melody. I know her, hazel eyes so bright. It was Raisha, but younger. I feel a tingling in my hands, and I look down at them. I always was invisible in all these little visions. I could see and feel myself and everything else, but no one else could see, or hear me. My

hands began to throb violently. A small kid in the ground shouted,
"There are hands floating there! Mommy, look!"
"Be quiet, Felicia."
Fade to black, fade to black, I thought and closed my eyes tight.
Everything faded away, just as I see a lady in a blue veil entering
the scene.

Safra opened her eyes to see Chuck, the Captain, Ahmed, Raisha, and Ridan peering down at her.

"Whew! You're alive!" Ridan shouted.

"Of course I am, dummy," she smiled.

"You fell off the cliff," the Captain said, "Chuck broke your fall."

"Thanks, Chuck," she grinned, and got up off the floor.

"Let's go, once again." The Captain said, relieved. Then they reached where the water started. Safra was fascinated by the way it seemed like a wall, where it abruptly stopped, like jelly. But when she put her hand inside, it went inside easily, the water cold to the touch. She let her whole body slip into the blue liquid. She felt her legs go through the same sensation, turning into a tail. She turned to see the others coming into the water, but Raisha hesitated.

"Raisha, come on!" Safra motioned her to come.

"I'm…I'm terrified of water," she said. "When I was imprisoned in the cave, there was no water at all!"

"I'll take you, come on." Safra took her hand, and began to swim towards the surface, but Ahmed and Raisha had not turned into seals. *Funny,* she thought.

She swam faster and faster, to make sure that Raisha would not lose her breath, and she finally broke the surface. She spotted a rope ladder going back up to the opening. "There's a ladder! Let's go!"

She dragged Raisha along with her, and as she stepped
out of the water, her tail disappeared. She clambered out
onto the soft grass, and the forest was gone. Sunshine
covered them like a thin, golden veil.
Safra breathed it in deeply. It never felt so good to just
stand in the warmth, with no worries at all.
  She sat down on the grass, and took out her notebook,
and began to write:

Safra's Log

June 11th, 4:53 pm.

*It's amazing about what can happen in a day. I think
there's a lot more to the mysterious girl, Raisha, than it
seems. I don't have much time to write, but there's one
thing. I had a vision, and instead of being invisible, my
hand started to solidify. A little girl from the vision saw
me! It was really weird and scary. I think it was
something of the past, because I saw Raisha very
differently. I've never done that before, and my visions are
changing.*

                                                    Safra

  She closed it. They had gone through many things, but it
hadn't even been a day since they had started. She quickly
put on her shoes.
  "We are setting up camp here for the night. It will get
dark soon," Ahmed said.
  Raisha rolled her eyes. "We know that, know-it-all," she
muttered.

Ahmed clenched his teeth and said, "At least you could come and help, lazy," he barked.

"How dare you…" Raisha rose up from her seat. "Calm down." Ridan snapped at her. He looked like he was going to give her a lecture about manners.

"Ridan, not now."

He frowned at Safra and walked away. She stared at Raisha, who refused to look back at her.

Safra sighed. This was not going well. Ahmed and Ridan didn't like Raisha, and she was important to their expedition too. Now, if Raisha left, all their clues would be gone. The rest of them didn't know how important it was to find out about Meera, Raisha definitely knew something about her. Safra sighed. What was next?

NINETEEN

THE PATH

Safra woke up to the sound of birds chirping. For a few minutes, she didn't get up and just stared at the ceiling. She hadn't slept very well, thinking about the whole situation. *I shouldn't be thinking about this. They must handle Raisha , even though they didn't like her. They should know how to adjust,* she thought. *I didn't do anything wrong, then why am I thinking about it?*

She threw back her covers, and walked out into the cold, damp, hazy morning. The rain had left the grass covered in droplets of sparkling dew, perfect in shape.

"Maybe I could take a walk," she murmured. The rest of them hadn't woken up.

She loved taking long walks alone. A path that she had never seen before looked so tempting to try. *I'll come back. I'll only go straight, and I'll leave a note for the rest of them.*

She quickly scribbled down a note, left it in Ridan's tent, and walked to the path.

Suddenly she noticed a silver colored creature down the road.

The white fox! It's trying to tell me something.
She started to run towards it, but what she saw made her
stop in her tracks.

It was no fox. A white, but almost silver albino peacock
stood in the middle of the road. It seemed to glow,
radiating so bright that Safra was sure that it could
probably outshine the sun. She closed her eyes, and the
peacock, sensing her presence, flew away. And as she
watched it disappear, a clinking sound of something
falling on the ground echoed through the air. Safra turned
to see a necklace, with a carved wooden whistle hanging
on it. Beautiful silver peacock feather designs etched on
it.

She clutched it in her hand. The eerie landscape finally
got to her, and she ran all the way back to the camp. Safra
made sure to remove the note from the tent, and then ran
back to hers. She had not known how hard she had held
the whistle in her hand. It had left sharp, red welts.

She wondered about what this meant. *I must discuss this
with the others, even the Captain. But would it be safe to show
Raisha? We don't know what she is capable of.* Safra was in a
dilemma once more. *That's one more mystery on our hands.*
She snuggled back into her covers, waiting for sunrise.
She sighed, and tried to fall asleep, but she could not. Her
mind was swirling with thoughts, like a cyclone. Finally,
out of sheer fatigue, she fell into a deep sleep. But as
soon as she had closed her eyes, it seemed as if the sun
had risen. *That's the way it goes,* she rolled her eyes, and got
up. She peered out to see Ahmed unpacking some
sandwiches, and Chuck roasting some on a freshly lit fire.
She got up and washed her face from her canteen. The
welts on her hands burned more than ever, but she

clenched them into fists as she walked up to Ahmed.
"Good morning, Safra," he smiled pleasantly.

"Ahmed, call the others. We need a meeting," she hissed,
making sure that Raisha wasn't anywhere in sight.

"Why?" he looked up at her questioningly.

"Just call the others!" She flashed her eyes. "We will
meet in my tent."

She ran back to her tent, and took out the whistle from
underneath her makeshift leaf pillow. It was beautiful, its
intricate designs glowing silver. Safra fingered the black
cord, tempted to wear it.

Ridan walked inside. "What did you call us about?" he
asked.

Chuck, the Captain, and Ahmed followed. "I made sure
Raisha was still in her tent," Chuck said.

"Thanks." Safra nodded in appreciation. "Okay. This is
what I wanted to show you," she said, and opened her
palm to reveal the whistle.

"Wow…" Ridan murmured. The Captain looked
surprised by her discovery. "When did you find this?" he
asked. "I went on an early morning walk, and I saw a
silvery white peacock on the path," she said.

"Silver, silver. There's a connection," Chuck said,
shaking his head.

"Anyways, it flew away when it saw me, and it left this. I
wonder why," Safra said.

Finally, after a few moments of silence, Chuck spoke up.
"We need to find out about this. There are too many
mysteries to be solved."

"What other mysteries?" the Captain asked. Of course he
didn't know about all the visions, Meera, and Zelda. "It's
time we tell him," Safra said. "Tell me what?" He looked
at them, waiting for an answer.

They narrated the whole story to him. "We're sorry we didn't trust you. I mean, you were just being…A little bit of a coward," Ridan stammered.

"No! I wasn't. I was a huge coward. And I'm sorry, all of you. I was just being such a jerk. I took all the credit. I am truly sorry, especially to Ahmed, who was so loyal to me." Everyone stood in shock.

Ahmed frowned. *Oh no, he might not accept his apology. This is going to be bad,* Safra thought. Ahmed's fear was distrust after all.

"Spoke like a true captain," he smiled, his expression changing. He and the Captain shook hands. *Oh. Maybe it's good after all.*

It was somewhat suspicious. Ahmed was only his shipmate, and most definitely not the Captain's friend.

Safra smiled anyway. It had been a long time since they had laughed and had a good time. She finally felt close to them, like they were her family.

She looked at Ridan from the corner of her eye. She would have to spend some time with him. She had a lot to do after this was over. *Adventure, just end already,* she thought.

Safra was so amazed that she had been so excited for this. Now all she wanted to do was to go home, and live a normal life. But now, she was a sailor. She needed to finish her duty.

TWENTY

THE HUNTERS

Safra cocked her head to the side. Voices were coming from Raisha's tent. "I guess it's time for me to pay her a little visit."

Safra slowly opened the flap in the cloth to see Raisha pacing around the room, saying, "Oh no, oh no, oh no, oh no," over and over again.

"Raisha, what's wrong?" Safra stepped into the tent, revealing herself.

She realized that Raisha had been crying.

"They are out to get me," she grasped Safra's hands in her own.

"Who? Who's out to get you?"

"The Hunters," she said in a hushed voice. "Look at this," she held out a note, written in wet, red ink. 'We are coming,' it read.

"How do you know who they are… these *Hunters*? And who are they anyway?" Safra asked.

"I have gotten notes from them before! You have to listen to me! We are all in danger," her grip on Safra tightened.

"Everyone, come on over here," Safra called out.

In seconds, they were all there.

"Listen to what Raisha has to say," she said.

"We are all in danger," Raisha showed them the note, and told them about the Hunters. They were a tribe who wore only black, and always covered their faces. They rode on fast, black horses, and had powerful weapons that could easily kill.

"Why are the Hunters after *you?*" Ridan asked rolling his eyes.

"That is not something you need to know right now. The problem is that the next place we pass, which is the Sun Oasis, is basically the Hunters' territory. They always patrol the area, and know that we will pass through it to get to the other side. They will surely kill us," she said. "They want me, mostly. But if you all are with me, they won't hesitate to kill you as well."

"Well, do they have a weakness? Maybe something we could use against them?" Ahmed asked.

"Well, it doesn't count as a weakness, but... They are very impatient. They won't find us if we hide ourselves and go slowly. They have sharp eyesight, so if we run, they will spot us easily. The Sun Oasis is a big place, and we won't get there as fast as you think. Maybe one or two days, according to our pace," Raisha said.

"How come you know all these stuff?" Chuck asked.

"I'm supposed to. Now listen. We need to make a plan. We need to hide from place to place, and we can't stay in the same place all the time or they will smell us out. Remember, the main thing is to not make no sound at all, and go slow," she said, "Got it?"

They all nodded as Raisha walked out of the tent to get her breakfast. "I wonder why the Hunters want her," Safra thought out loud.

"That's what all of us are wondering," Chuck said.
"Mm," Ridan looked like he was thinking hard about
something. Safra peeked out of the tent to see Raisha
helping herself to sandwiches. Whenever Safra looked at
her, she felt a bit of jealousy. Oh, what she would have
done to have a mysterious past! Raisha was so young, yet
so experienced.
"Well, crew, we got to get moving to the Sun Oasis,"
said the Captain. "Gather all the supplies."
They worked for an hour to pack everything, and they
drew out the maps. Raisha was in a world of her own,
sitting on a log, staring at a tree. No one seemed to mind
her, but Safra couldn't help but take a small glance
occasionally.
"It's time for us to embark on the next part of our
quest," the Captain said.
Safra turned her head to see a tropical forest in the
distance. "I thought there was a desert."
"Oh, it used to be. But, a very powerful sorceress used it,
and enchanted it. It made the desert into a beautiful
forest," Raisha replied.
Sorceress? There sure are some crazy people here.
They trekked to the entrance of the forest, where they
stood in silence. It looked warm and welcoming, but they
knew what hid deep inside. The Hunters.
"Let's go," Safra said.
"First hiding place will be those hedges. We can fit
underneath them," Raisha pointed. Very slowly, they
crawled under the hedges. Safra heard something rustling
in the leaves. "Guys," she whispered.
"I know, I heard it. Keep quiet, and stay still," Raisha
whispered. They did not move a muscle, and suddenly,
black hooves rushed past them, as fast as lightning.

The Hunters.

Many other pairs of black hooves thundered past, making war cries. The six of them trembled in fear.

After the sounds died away, they slowly shifted to big tree hollows, and then behind rocks. It went on for hours and hours. They were exhausted, with no excuses to eat or drink, drained of their morale.

"I can't do this anymore," Ridan groaned. "Me neither," Safra slumped onto the ground.

"We must go on," the Captain said, and helped them get up. They trudged all the way to a place surrounded by trees by the waterfall. "We must find the Oasis. If you drink the water, you may become invisible. If we reach it, we can easily avoid them the rest of the way," Raisha said. "Well you didn't say that before! Let's go!" Safra got up from her seat.

"Yes, but there is still a long way to go, even if it is in the middle of the forest," Raisha said.

"Okay, but do we still have to do this?" Safra said, her forehead wrinkling in disgust.

"Do what?" Ridan asked.

"You know, hiding from them." She looked hopefully at Raisha.

"No! Remember? Raisha said they can easily find and kill you! That's the only way," Ahmed said, turning to look at Raisha, who remained silent.

"But what if we fight? We have the weapons too!" Safra retaliated, giving Ridan a look that meant: *Come on. Say something.*

He shook his head no. "Safra! Are you crazy?" Chuck said, alarmed.

"No. I'm not," she said. "I'm tired of you all treating me like I'm crazy! The last time you said that, my plan worked. We're in a place that anything could happen. And only *crazy* ideas are going to work out now." Safra exploded.

"That's the point. We don't know what's going to happen. That's where Raisha comes in. She knows about all of this stuff, and we need to listen to her," the Captain raised his eyebrows.

"She's right," Raisha said.

Everyone stopped talking and arguing, and stared at Raisha in awe. "Safra's right. We must fight. This has gone on too long," she said, and raised a sword from her belt. "Yeah!" Chuck raised a machete.

"Yeah!" Ridan unsheathed a dagger from his belt. Safra took out a bow and a quiver of arrows, and slung it on her shoulder. "Let's fight," she said. Even the Captain took out his sword. "Let's go, I guess," he said. The Captain didn't seem very enthusiastic about the idea, but he also didn't want to let his crew down. He hadn't fought for years, and now he was against a bunch of ruthless people who could kill him easily. "That's the way it goes," he muttered.

"EEYAH EEYAH!" Ridan shouted out a battle cry of his own and charged out into the forest. But, the problem was, none of the Hunters were in sight. "They aren't here," Safra murmured.

"They will surprise you. Don't keep your guard down," Raisha whispered.

They stood in silence, trying to find them amongst the trees.

"AAAAAAAH!" Chuck shouted, shattering the silence. He fell on the ground, motionless.

"Chuck!" Safra shouted. "No time! Safra, look behind you!" Safra whirled around and fired, wounding the

Hunter that had tried to attack her. She ran towards Ridan, who was battling two of them at once, and fired once more.

They kept fighting, for hours and hours, but the Hunters had much better stamina. As they became tired, the Hunters grew stronger.

Safra dropped to the ground. She was exhausted, dripping with sweat, and she was running out of arrows. She needed to get back to the waterfall and get some more, but there were Hunters everywhere.

She was lost. She could see her friends, but not the waterfall. *I must help in the battle, and I must find Chuck.* She raced over to Ahmed's side to help him. It went on and on. The Hunters kept coming, one by one. Six people could not subdue them, let alone escape alive. She knew she had to do something.

Surprisingly, she could also see Chuck fighting, with no injuries. First, she had to get to the cave to refill her quiver. She watched the Hunters disperse, heading towards another direction. In the distance, she spotted the waterfall. "Ridan! I need backup!" she shouted. "Clear my path!"

He jumped into the way and held off the Hunters. Their attention was drawn to him, and Safra sprinted to the cave. She dashed to grab more arrows, but she spotted something more interesting. Spilling out of Ahmed's bag were…Oranges. Fresh, ripe…Oranges.

She then began to burrow furiously into his bag. She threw out of the contents on the floor, shifting through them like a hungry dog looking for something to eat. She finally found what she was looking for: a box of matches. Something had clicked, deep in the back of her mind. She gathered as many as possible, and filled her quiver with it.

Armed, she ran outside, towards the Hunters. One of them had already spotted her, and steadied his bow. Safra's deft fingers ripped off a piece of the orange skin and struck a match, lighting the peel on fire. She hurled it right at him as hard as she could, and his robes began to glow with flames. Quickly brushing off the peel, he shouted, "Retreat!" The voice sounded peculiar. She noticed that this was the only Hunter that wore a helmet, with sharp metal spikes. He lifted the helmet, clutching it tightly, and let the aflame robe float away in the wind.

"Retreat!" Long, black hair billowed out of the helmet. The Hunter turned around to face them, her pale face glowing in the sunlight. Her eyes, one green, the other icy blue, flashed at Safra. But she looked just like…*Meera! Is that her? She looks just like her! But no, she has different eyes and black hair. But…But…That face...*

Safra took out another piece of orange peel menacingly, giving her a warning. *Go away from my friends. Go away. Get out of my life, or you are facing more of these.*

She kept throwing them at the Hunters until they finally retreated.

They had finally chased them away. The Hunters were gone. "Whoo-hoo! We have defeated them!" Ridan shouted in victory.

"AHHHH!" Safra suddenly shouted in pain and clutched her shoulder, and fell to the ground. An arrow had grazed her, leaving a large cut.

"Safra!" Ridan rushed to her side. Ahmed glanced behind them, spotting a Hunter running away.

"It almost happened to Chuck. He freaked out and screamed, but it didn't hit him. Are you okay?" the Captain asked, kneeling next to her.

"It's not so bad. It didn't hit her completely, only grazed her. She will be okay," said Chuck, pressing a wet cloth to the cut.

"I guess I'm fine now," she murmured. She stood up slowly, still holding her shoulder tightly. She took a deep breath. "Let's go," she said. "We need to find the Oasis, and we need to find it soon."

TWENTY-ONE

SAFRA'S VISION

They had gathered all of their supplies, and had set out towards the Sun Oasis. The bright, hot sun beat down on them, sweat running down their foreheads. Somehow, their bags felt heavier.

"Oh boy, how I would love to take a nap right now," Ridan panted. Safra did not say anything back. She felt like there was a pit in her stomach, giving her an uneasy feeling. Her shoulder throbbed, and she clutched it tighter. She glanced at the cloth wrapped around it, now stained with red. Her knees buckled from underneath her, and she dropped to the ground.

I feel fresh, like I just woke up from a deep sleep. A musty smell fills the room. I stare at the place I am in. I am standing in a beautiful, black stone corridor, adorned with beautiful silver ornaments. I brush my hand along the smooth walls, exploring every crack and crevice. Somehow, I knew that something was important about this place. Words crept into my mind: Rose Scepter, curse, silver. They overlapped, creating a mass of voices whispering in my head. I try to shake it off, but it doesn't work. But in a way, I was drawn to the voices. I wanted to listen to what they were saying. I strained my ear, trying as hard as I could to hear them. But those three words kept circling around in my head, making everything else inaudible.

A large door stands in front of my way. I stare at the stained glass that decorates it. I jiggle the lock, and of course, it does not work. I raise my foot, and it smashes through the glass. How did I do that? I had never displayed my power like that before. I watched the colored shards fall on the floor. I stepped through the jagged hole I had just created, and entered a room, completely covered in silken black cloth, covered in silver print. I see a table in the center of the room, an object covered in cloth sitting on it. I start walking towards it, but something makes me stop. I hear footsteps. Someone was coming! But they can't see me, could they? The same tingling feeling washes over me. Oh no. This means I'm becoming solid again. The steps become louder with every second. My eyelids immediately seem to glue themselves together. I wait, and wait, and wait.

Everything fades.

Safra opened her eyes to see Raisha, Ridan, Chuck, Ahmed, and the Captain bending over her. "She's awake!" Ridan shouted.

Safra got up. Surprisingly, her shoulder did not hurt as much. She felt as fresh as she had in her vision. "I'm fine," she insisted.

"You've been lying down here for at least an hour." Ridan said.

What? But… Whenever I have a vision, it only lasts for a few seconds in real time. The vision lasts longer. But it's different now. Something is wrong…

"I said I'm fine," she said. "Let's get going." "But…" Chuck stammered. "I *said*, let's get going."

Ridan walked beside her. "If you're looking for an explanation, I had a vision," she said, tired of everyone fussing over her. "But, it lasted for over an hour. It can't be a vision. Something's wrong, and you're not well," Ridan protested.

"Yes! Something is wrong. Remember when I fell off the rock wall when we rescued Ahmed? A girl from the vision saw my hands, after they started to tingle. The same thing happened again this time and now the visions are lengthening. You don't believe me?" she asked in grouchy tone.

"Really? I mean — that couldn't be true…"

"Fine. I'll find someone else who'll believe me." Safra sped up and left Ridan speechless. He sighed. "Safra!" he called out after her.

Safra felt a hot droplet of water cascade down her cheek. She was tired of it. She felt like everyone was acting like she was crazy, and never believed her. She felt a warm, gentle hand on her back. She quickly wiped the tears off her face and turned to face Raisha.

"I know how it feels. Trust me," Raisha whispered, quickening her pace to keep up with Safra.

"What do you mean?" Safra asked.

"I can see it in you. You're a Seer, right?" she said.

"How did you know?"

"You are wearing a locket. I was born and raised here, and I am something different too. I'm a Healer."

"Healer means…"

"I can heal things, but only small things, like cuts, or bruises. I'm developing it, though. Ridan can do something too, right?" she asked.

"Yes. He knows how to read other languages, and can communicate with animals," she said, astonished.

"I knew it! Of course he would be a Whisperer. Yes, yes, of course," she mumbled to herself. "What? What do you mean?" Safra asked.

"I'll explain soon."

"Tell me now."

"If I tell you now, you'll only have more questions." Safra sighed. She knew that she was inquisitive. She always had questions, and she had to know the answer, even if they were obvious.

"Here, leave it to me," Raisha said, and removed the cloth from Safra's shoulder. She placed her hands on the cut, and a green light managed to squeeze itself through her fingers. Safra turned to look at the cut, now only a white scar. She would not forget this, ever. She would not leave the island without solving this, and getting back at those Hunters.

"How did you do that?"

"I told you. I'm a Healer, so I have green light magic. You are a Seer, so you have blue light magic. Ridan is a Whisperer, so he has red light magic. Look," she said, and took out a locket that looked exactly like Safra's, except the obsidian stone was shaped like a leaf.

"Safra!" Ahmed's voice echoed through the air.

"I'll tell you more. I promise," Raisha took Safra's hands in her own, and slipped away.

Safra wondered about what Raisha had told her. *Magic? Raisha is a Healer? What does this all mean? Why does this have to be so confusing?*

TWENTY-TWO

CHUCK'S GONE

"What were you doing, talking to Raisha? You know we can't trust her," Ahmed said crossly.

"What do you mean? What harm could she do?" Safra frowned.

"We don't know who she is. Look at the Hunters. They wounded you. What if she did something like that?" he insisted. "Speaking of your injury…You took the cloth off. But how…How did it…" he stammered.

"You don't understand Raisha. She's perfectly fine. She healed my cut. You see, she has a locket like me, and she has healing powers. It's unbelievable." Safra's smile faded.

"You probably don't believe me, right?"

"Yes, I'm afraid so! You probably healed it, in some way. Still, Raisha should not be trusted," Ahmed said. He still could not accept that Raisha was a good person. The Captain walked up to them.

"Hey, I'm the Captain. I give the orders around here," he glared at Ahmed. "Yes, we should be careful around her. But she has some good abilities, like wielding a sword, which could be of aid. She has not betrayed us, and she warned us about the Hunters. She helped fight them. She is not dangerous, but be cautious." Safra liked that. The Captain had been fair.

"I agree with the Captain," Chuck said.

"I still say we should we have to stay away from her," Ahmed muttered.

Safra frowned. He simply did not like Raisha. But what about Ridan?

Safra knew that Ridan really liked Ahmed, and looked up at him. He did not want to disagree with Ahmed, even though he probably wanted to support Chuck and the Captain. Safra turned to him, expecting him to pick Ahmed's side, but he did not say anything.

"How did your cut heal so fast?" the Captain asked. "Whatever," she muttered. She wanted to stray away from that topic. The Captain and Ahmed walked away, talking between themselves.

"Safra—Maybe it is true…" Ridan walked up to her.

"And you still don't," she said. "Nobody believes me, except Raisha. And you don't like her either, just because Ahmed doesn't like her. Think for yourself, Ridan. Don't follow someone else's way of thinking."

"I am not!"

"Yes you are."

"Well you're the crazy one!"

"I'm not crazy!"

"Yes you are!"

"Fine. You called me crazy, didn't you? Now let's see what happens," she said, and stomped away.

She caught up to Raisha. "Now even my brother is calling me crazy," she sighed. "Ahmed doesn't trust you, I'm sorry to say."

"That's okay. He'll learn to trust me."

"So…"

"We need to keep going. According to my calculations, the Sun Oasis is somewhere near here. Keep your eyes peeled," Raisha said, holding out a compass, and headed to the left.

Safra felt a rush of fresh air, her long hair flapping in the wind. She breathed in the tropical, fruity scent.

Her instincts told her that it was nearby. "Oh! Yes! We're here!" Raisha began to run towards the origin of the sweet fumes. "Can you smell that?! And look, palm trees! We're here!"

Safra followed Raisha, dashing through bushes and trees. They reached an empty pit, streaked with cracks, indicating that it had once held water. It was surrounded by the palm trees they had seen earlier.

"But wait. It's an oasis, right? There's no water! What is this? I told you she tricked us!" Ahmed had finally found a reason to try and find a simple fault with her.

"Calm down, Ahmed. Watch and learn." Raisha said calmly. She walked to a tree, and tapped the trunk three times. The ground beneath them started to rumble, nearly knocking them to the ground. "AAAH!" Chuck shouted, tumbling into the pit.

"Chuck!" Safra shouted. She tried to get up, but she could not. She started to crawl on her hands and knees, trying to reach the pit, but the rumbling and the shaking prevented her to move.

Suddenly, the cracks began filling with fresh, clean water. Safra's eyes glassed over as she stared at it, her throat longing for it. Her mouth was already imagining the sweet taste of the crystal-clear water.

The water rose higher and higher, and Chuck was engulfed by the liquid, forming a whirlpool. Ridan screamed. "Chuck! Chuck! CHUCK!"

The Captain freaked out.

Safra broke out of her reverie, and got ready to jump into the water. She crouched down low and pressed her hands together, her head bent. She let her feet drop, allowing herself to fall headfirst into the oasis.

But, she never felt the cool water. A strong hand held her waist, preventing Safra to dive.

"Raisha! What are you doing?"

"Trust me. He'll come up."

And, as she had said, he surfaced, coughing and spluttering.

"Spit! Spit the water out. Don't drink it!" Raisha warned. Chuck did as he was told, and swam back to them. "That was scary," he said.

"Phew! That was close," Safra let out a sigh of relief. Safra bent down to take a sip of water, when Raisha shouted, "No! Don't!" She grabbed Safra by the shirt and pulled her up. "Why not?" Safra asked.

"One drop will be enough. If you drink too much, you'll probably be invisible for years," she explained. "Some people have done it, and are still missing."

"But I'm thirsty! And our water supply is going lower and lower," Safra protested.

"Here," Raish a slowly dripped one drop of water into Safra's mouth. Her thirst was immediately quenched, and she felt like she never needed to drink water again. "Safra! You're invisible! It worked!" Ridan shouted. Safra looked down at herself, but she could still see herself."Hmmm, she murmured. "I can hear you though, Ridan piped up. Safra turned to see Chuck gulping down the water in large chugs, "Finally," he groaned happily.

"No! Chuck! Didn't you hear what Raisha said?"
Safra shouted, her eyes widening.

"Huh?" he looked up, and seemed to fade away
into the sky.

"He's invisible," Ridan said.

"Forever invisible, you mean! Oh no!" Raisha
started to pace around the oasis.

"Now what?" the Captain looked worried.
"Chuck isn't going to reappear? What about
Safra?"

"She will reappear in thirty minutes or so. But
Chuck…This can only mean one thing," Raisha
muttered to herself.

"Everyone, I know what to do. Drink a drop of
the water, and fill some extra canteens with the
water. The Hunters might come back, and I know
how to cure Chuck. We must go on, and face the
next obstacle, the Rede Mountains."

TWENTY-THREE

THE REDE MOUNTAINS

She took a deep breath. *Don't panic. Chuck will be fine.* The invisibilty had worn off of Safra, so they had made sure to make Chuck wear a jacket so they would know where he was. They also had instructed to him to talk from time to time, just to make sure.

Safra was worried about him, and Raisha wouldn't tell her anything. *She's hiding something from me. I hope she's right, that she can cure Chuck. But, maybe, she just said that so the others wouldn't freak out. I have no idea.*

They soon exited the forest, and a blast of frigid air hit them like a bullet. Safra could hardly open her eyes, but she already knew where they were. They had reached the Rede Mountains.

As the wind slowly lessened, Safra opened her eyes, only to see a massive range of snowy peaks towering in front of her. *I wonder why I didn't see these before,* she wondered. "I didn't see these on our way here!" the invisible Chuck said, as if reading her mind.

"That's because there's a heavy fog. You can't see them from far away," Raisha answered.

"I remember seeing a fog," the Captain said. Ahmed stayed silent, staring at the white, gloomy landscape. *What's wrong with him? Maybe it's because of Raisha,* she thought.

One day, they were on an adventure to find the silver sand, and now, they had to find a way to get Chuck back to normal. All this drama had made them forget why they had come here in the first place. *But why did Raisha come? Because she is on some type of quest, right? Maybe she's on the same quest as we are on!* Safra suddenly remembered that she had seen these mountains as she had been sailing around the island, and she had seen a black creature walking across the snow. She closed her eyes and tried to remember how it looked like, but her memory seemed to fail her. Her mind raced frantically, rewinding back to the time after the storm.

Safra sighed. She could not remember. She dug her hands into her pockets, and felt the small leather notebook in the back of her pocket. She hadn't written in it for a while. Time seemed to go by as slow as possible, and Safra's motivation seems to have drained out of her.

"I...Can't...Go...On," Ridan groaned.

"What?" Safra turned around.

"I'm so tired," he said, and sat down on the ground. His eyes were bloodshot, and his knuckles were icy white.

"I'm exhausted too," she admitted, and sat down next to him.

"Ok, break time, I guess," the Captain plopped down as well. Suddenly, he cried, "AH! Chuck! You sat on my leg!"

Safra chuckled as she could see a jacket hovering next to the Captain. "Oh, sorry," Chuck teased, a hint of mischief in his voice. Although she could not see him, she could already imagine how his expression looked like.

"That's not funny, Chuck," the Captain grumbled.

"Yes it is."

"Cut it out, you two!" Safra chuckled.

"Fine…" Chuck muttered.

"Everyone, put on your coats," Raisha said. Safra dug into her rucksack to find the coat Zelda had given her. She fingered the glass beads woven into the fur. Safra hugged it against herself, taking in all the warmth. Her eyelids drooped, and using the coat as a pillow, she closed her eyes.

As I closed my eyes, I see a familiar place. A crackling fire with a peacock mantelpiece hangs near my feet. It was Zelda's cabin. I was back there again. I was seeing the past.

I see her in the fire again. I can see Meera, with her streaked jet-black hair and green and blue eyes. Wait.

Streaked jet-black hair? Green and blue eyes? No. It can't be. But now I realize that I had not seen Meera, only that weird lady who was probably the leader of the Hunters. I had confused myself.

The Hunter lady was the one who I had to defeat.

But what had she done that bad?

All I knew was that she was dangerous. She was after Raisha and now us as well. I decided that I would avoid her as much as possible, and first I would finish my quest. My vision blurs, and I blink a few times before closing them.

"Safra…Safra! Wake up!"

"Huh?"

"Wake up!"

"She sat up to see Ridan above her. *Oh no.*

"C'mon. Let's head to the mountains," he said, and held out a hand. Safra took it and stood up.

He hadn't noticed that she had been in a vision, and
Safra kept it that way. She turned towards the high,
majestic peaks. The snow looked like sugar that had been
freshly sifted on gray rock candy. "Come on everyone!"
the Captain shouted, and they began walking along a path
that went between the mountains.

TWENTY-FOUR

THE PANTHER

They trudged through the cold path. Large peaks towered over them like giants.

Safra rubbed her arms, hoping that it would help her feel warmer. She stared at the foggy road that lay before her, slightly intimidated by the distance ahead. *I wonder what we're going to face now.*

"Let's keep going, team," the Captain said awkwardly, trying to boost their morale. Ahmed just sighed.

Safra sped up to catch up with Ahmed. "What's up? You look really...Down in the dumps."

He sighed again, but now it was getting on Safra's nerves. "Aren't you going to tell me anything?"

"The Captain is in danger."

"What?"

"You'll find out," he said, and smiled wistfully at her before walking away.

"I'll ask the Captain, then," Safra muttered. She edged past Raisha and Ridan, and yelled, "Captain!"

"Shhhh. Be quiet, there could be an avalanche," he whispered.

"But…Captain…"

"Not now," he said, cocking his ear to the right.

"Captain…"

"Safra! I said not now. I hear something," he said.

"Captain! There…"

"Can't you listen? I said not now!"

"There's something over there!"

He turned to see something disappear behind a rock, and immediately unsheathed his sword. "Everyone, don't let your guard down," he said. Safra equipped herself with her bow and arrow, and Raisha, Chuck, Ridan, and Ahmed armed themselves as well.

Raisha's watchful eyes caught a black figure lurking in the shadows. "There!" she shouted, pointing at a cliff. "We must go up there!" she shouted. A dark, small route led to the top. "Let's do it!" Safra agreed, but the rest seemed to differ.

"It's too dangerous to go up there! Are you crazy?" Ahmed shouted through all the wind and snow. "We'll die!"

"We're not crazy!" Safra finally lost it. "What else do you expect us to do then? Why don't you think of ideas for a change?"

"Okay, fine! I suggest we forget about this black *thingy* and go on!"

"Ahmed…Remember…" the Captain said softly, "they're right."

"Oh, yes Captain. I remember. I'm sorry," he muttered.

"Then let's go up on that cliff!" the Captain shouted, once again becoming awkward.

Safra frowned at Ahmed before following the Captain through the dark path. *Crazy. That word again. Is that what I am? Am I crazy?*

Safra turned to face the Captain. "Captain?"
"Yes?"
"Ahmed told me about something…"
"I know. You will find out, or I will tell you."
"When?"
"I will soon, if I survive."
Safra sighed. It was the same answer as she had got before. *You will find out soon, blah blah blah.*

As they went deeper into the darkness, it became colder and colder, and the wind became stronger and stronger. Safra had to squint just to see.

The path started to slope upwards. Safra could feel the roughly carved stone steps through her shoes. She looked over the edge, only to be surprised about how high they actually were. The peaks looked smaller, and the road looked like a tiny line. *We were actually there, walking, a few minutes ago,* she thought and smiled. *Wow.*

She turned to see the Captain looking very nervous. It was so cold, but perspiration ran down his forehead like a waterfall.

"Captain? What's wrong?" Safra asked.
They had reached the cliff. "That." He whispered, and pointed to the black creature standing there. "The panther."

It turned to face them, shaking off delicate snowflakes off its coat. Its sleek black fur was mesmerizing; its eyes scanning them head to toe.

This is the black creature I saw!
They finally focused on the Captain, and its mouth curved into a snarl and advanced slowly towards him. Gradually, its pace quickened, until it turned into a fast run. Its sharp claws were bared.

Safra's mind was whirring with thoughts. *Should I jump in front of the Captain and save him? Or should I try fire my arrows? No, I can't do that, I would probably miss. Oh no! What if I fail?* She finally decided about what she would do. She started to run. She stood in front of the Captain, closed her eyes, and prepared to die.

"Safra!" Ridan screamed. "Stop!" He saw the panther leap towards her.

But, before it hit her, a silver glow radiated through her body, and the panther slid right through Safra. The light faded, but she had failed to save him!

But just in time, he wounded it with his sword, and it fell down to the ground.

"Go away! Leave us alone," the Captain bellowed.

The injured animal flashed its eyes at him, and leaped off the cliff. It cleanly landed on its feet on another rock, and disappeared.

"Go Captain! You have done it, my friend!" Ahmed cheered.

"Yes!" Safra hugged him in ecstasy. "But how did it jump over me?"

"It didn't jump over you! It went through you!" Ridan exclaimed.

"What?" she was dumbfounded. "I can explain that," the Captain said. "I have a confession to make, everyone," the Captain hung his head in embarrassment.

"What confession?" they all asked in unison.

"Well, it's a long story."

TWENTY-FIVE

THE CAPTAIN'S CONFESSION

All of them sat down in a circle, while Ahmed gathered kindling for a small fire. The Captain cleared his throat and began.

"Once I was a young sailor. I had just been recruited on The Ships, and…"

"You were recruited before you became captain?"

"Well, of course! Now, let me finish, Safra. I have lied to all of you, but it is all for good reason. Ahmed was my younger shipmate, and we were good friends. That year, we actually found Silver Island, and Ahmed and I ventured out on our own. That's when we entered this mountain range."

"But how come you didn't know about the other obstacles, or the star Polaris?"

"That was a long time ago, so the island must have changed a lot. Moving on, yes, we entered this mountain range, and we encountered this panther. And I acted like I was the leader, because I was older. But Ahmed was much more mature and braver than me, but I refused to accept it. And, as if knowing that I was the cowardly one, the panther dove for me. I was foolish. I stood there, frightened, and that's how I got this," he said, motioning to the scar on his face. "I was frozen. But, thanks to Ahmed, I am alive. I was so thankful to him. But I was also very embarrassed, and when we went back to the crew, they found out about what had happened. They all laughed at me," he continued. "But sadly, our ship was destroyed, by another small hurricane on the island. We returned to Erina in rowboats, and we could not remember what route we took because our documents were washed away with the ship. At that time, we had calculated our route because we didn't have the map."

"Wow," Safra whispered.

"A few years later, I created a new crew. I started The Ships all over again, and I became captain. But, still, remembering that embarrassing event, I did not reveal my name to anyone. I am almost sad to say that I am Captain Henry Royce of The Ships."

There was only silence.

Safra stuttered, "Wow." Her mouth fell open in shock. She had thought of the Captain as a coward, and she had been right, but not anymore. The more time she spent with him, she realized he had a personality like none other.

She got up from the ground and hugged him tightly. "I'm sorry Captain," she whispered enough so he could not hear her.

"Captain, but why would you tell us, of all people?" Ridan asked.

"I trust you all," was his answer.

"Captain, should we tell Raisha about the peacock whistle? She might know something about it," Safra whispered to him.

"Yes, I believe she is trustworthy, after all, she does know a lot about this island," he said and gave her a wan smile.

She took it out of her bag. "Raisha, there's something you might want to see," she said, and opened her fist.

Raisha gasped. "When did you get this?"

"Before we faced the Hunters."

"Did you see Dayak?"

"Dayak?"

"He's a white peacock. Did you see him?"

"Yes, a peacock dropped the whistle there," Safra replied.

"Oh no! We must get going! We probably will face a serious danger. The whistle is vital," she said. "Let's go!" Without giving an explanation about what she was talking about, she gathered all her things, and began to walk down the stone steps. "Come on everyone!"

Safra rubbed her hands together, savoring the last of the fire's heat, before Ahmed threw snow on it.

"Let's go, Safra," he said, and they walked together down the steps.

No one spoke a word. There was an occasional cough or a sneeze, but other than that, there was no sound at all. Safra decided to talk to Ahmed.

"Hey, Ahmed?"

"Yeah?"

"I never knew that you and the Captain were friends."

"Of course you didn't."

"But then why did the Captain become captain and not you? He said you were the brave one."

"That's another difference between Henry and me. He was a very determined person with big dreams. Even though I had the guts and the ability, I was quite content with a lazy life. But, no, Henry needed adventure, and he wanted it to be interesting. Plus, his father was the captain before him," he explained, and his eyes filled with a nostalgic look. Safra had never heard him call the Captain by his actual name.

"Wow, I never knew that you both had such a deep, long history together." she said.

"Even I can't believe it."

Safra sighed. New obstacles, new enemies, and new secrets were being revealed one by one, while others remained mysteries. What else would they face?

TWENTY-SIX

SURROUNDED

They had walked quite a distance, and they soon reached a fork in the road. One led up into the mountain, and the other continued into the path.

"Which one should we take?" Ridan asked the Captain. "I don't think that going higher into the mountains are going to take us anywhere," the Captain said. "We'll go the other way," he said.

Safra stared at the mountain path. It twisted and turned around the peak, making it look somewhat like an ice cream cone. "Safra! Let's go!" Ahmed shouted.

As she turned to answer him, her eyes caught a silvery figure standing next to the root of the other path. It was the white fox!

"Hi there," Safra said, but she did not approach it.

It started to whimper, motioning to the other path.

"Guys, wait! Maybe…We should take this path," she said. The fox seemed to nod.

"Safra! Quit stalling! Let's go!" Ridan yelled.

"I can't do anything now," she whispered as she followed the others, who were way ahead. But somehow, she wondered if she had made a grave mistake.

As they walked down the path, the air seemed to grow thinner, making it harder to breathe. Snow began to fall harder. The cold air twisted around them like a thick, strangling scarf.

"I'm thinking that we should have taken the other path," Safra said, shouting against the powerful wind. It was becoming darker and darker.

"Don't be ridiculous! It would be colder up there!" the Captain shouted back.

"I didn't mean the cold!" Safra yelled.

"Then what did you mean?" the Captain yelled back.

"I— I just don't think that this was the right choice!"

"What? I can't hear you!" the Captain shouted.

"Huh?" Safra squinted.

"What?"

"What did you say?"

"Cut it out, both of you!" Raisha shouted. "Huh?" the Captain and Safra shouted in unison.

"Keep quiet!"

"Everyone! I hear something!" Ridan shouted.

All of them stopped walking and remained silent. Through all the wind, they could not hear anything.

"I can't hear anything!" Raisha shouted.

"Shhhh. Be quiet and listen!" Silence.

"Wait…"

Safra closed her eyes. A low, deep growling sound rang through her ears.

"I can hear it," Chuck whispered to Safra.

Something was there.

"I can too. I knew we shouldn't have taken this route!" Safra whispered back.

"What do you mean by that?"

"I'll explain later."

The sounds became louder and louder. Safra was thinking hard. *What is going on?*

It's some kind of animal of something like that. It doesn't sound like the panther. Something…Different. What if it's something another creature? Was it the hyenas again?

The snowy fog began to part, Safra strained to see what it was.

Large, smoky shadows started to become clear, and eerie, glowing eyes stared at them. There were six snow leopards, ready to pounce!

"Oh, great. This is just great. Snow leopards," Chuck muttered.

They began to advance, pushing the six of them back, until they bumped into each other. The leopards moved, forming a perfect circle.

They were surrounded.

TWENTY-SEVEN

SAFRA'S CRAZY AND BRILLIANT PLAN

"What are we going to do now?" Ridan hissed. "How should I know?" Safra hissed back. "You're the one with the crazy…"

Safra gave him a warning look.

"The one with the crazy *and brilliant* plans," he finished.

"That's better."

"Don't waste our time!"

"I'm thinking about some ideas right now!"

"Yeah, yeah, I can hear the gears running and whirring in your head."

"Ridan, stop it!" Safra clenched her fist inside her pocket. Inside her palm, she could feel a small wooden object. It was the peacock whistle!

A sudden thought struck her.

She took the whistle out, placed it in her mouth, and blew into it as hard as she could. A melodious sound filled the air, and it sounded like a thousand beautiful songs mixed together. A feeling of euphoria swept across Safra as the snowy wind began to swirl around and around, and then it stopped, revealing a beautiful white creature. The leopards used their paws to hide their eyes from the bright light.

"Dayak, it's you!" Raisha shouted happily and hugged the white peacock tightly.

"Ah! That's tight!"

"Did that peacock just speak?" the Captain looked like he would faint. "I'm going crazy!"

Safra's mouth was wide open. Ridan was rubbing his eyes. Chuck touched the peacock's feathers to make sure it was real.

"Don't touch me, I'm sensitive!" Dayak squawked.

"Whoa!" Chuck whispered.

"The light is going to fade! The leopards are going to come after us!" Safra said.

"What are you waiting for? Run!" the Captain said and wasted no time. He took off on full speed.

Raisha grabbed Dayak and all of them copied him, running as fast as they could. The light faded, and leopards knew that the game was up. Safra knew that the chances of escape were low.

"Dayak, help us! Help! Do something!" she shouted.

"What do you mean? I'm not your servant that's supposed to help you!" He looked rather offended.

"Ahem! That's *exactly* what you're supposed to be!" Raisha shouted at him.

"No, I'm not!"

"Yes you are! Now, *stop arguing with me!*"

"I won't!"

"You're supposed to listen to me!"

"I know, I know," Dayak muttered sarcastically. Raisha lost it. She grabbed him by the neck and stared deep into his beady eyes.

"You…Are…Supposed…To….LISTEN!" she yelled.

"Got it?"

He gulped. "Yes ma'am."

"Now do something!"

He closed his eyes, stopped running, and sat down on the ground.

"You are one weird bird! You're…You're going to get eaten! The leopards are coming! What in the world are you doing?" Safra shouted at him, running slowly.

"I'm trying to wish upon a star to save us."

"What?" Safra stopped.

"Star light, star bright, first star I see tonight, I wish I may, I wish I might, have the wish I wish tonight," he murmured.

"Come on, you silly bird! The rest of them are running away! We're going to get eaten!" Safra panicked. They were surely dead meat.

The leopards were close, but Dayak did not move.

"Please, grant my wish, my queen."

A tinkling sound of bells rung through the air, and all the stars in the night sky formed the shape of a smiling Meera. The light shone down upon them, creating an ice wall between them and the leopards. The others stopped in their tracks. A tear glistened in Raisha's eye.

"You haven't done that in a long time," Raisha clapped Dayak on his back. "Wait. Not that you've done anything like that before."

"You saved our lives," Safra said gratefully.

"I know!" he said, smiling proudly.

The Captain frowned at his attitude. "So we're stuck with this…*parrot* for the rest of this adventure?" he asked grouchily.

"I could always send him back…" Raisha started.

"First of all, I'm a peacock, and second, don't send me back! If you do, I can't come out until you summon me again, unless it's for a few minutes. I just saved your lives!"

"I know!" the Captain imitated his squeaky voice.

Dayak gave him an intense glare.

"If looks could kill," the Captain snickered.

Dayak opened his beak, but closed it again. He frowned at the Captain. "Pah! I'll take care of *you* later!" he muttered.

TWENTY-EIGHT

NIGHTTIME

"Raisha," Safra said, "How can he talk?"

"He's a magical peacock, of course," she said, "didn't you see that already?"

"Yeah…I kind of figured that out," she replied, feeling embarrassed.

"Let's get going. We have a long way ahead of us," Ahmed said. "Let's go!"

"Yeah, let's go."

They resumed their path, and soon they reached a small thicket. "Let's spend the night here," Safra said, and flopped down onto the ground and threw off her rucksack.

"No time to waste. Get to work!" the Captain ordered. "Pitch the tents!"

"Ugh. Fine." Safra groaned and stood up. Ahmed handed her a tent.

After setting up camp, Safra took out her notebook. "What's that?" Dayak squawked.

"It's a notebook," she said, swiping it away from his reach.

"I can see that, but what do you use it for?"
"Nothing, I just write down stuff about my adventures."
"Can I see?"
 "No, sorry."
"Why not?"
"I just want to keep it personal."
"So?"
"That's why I won't show you!"
"What?"
"Go away, you silly bird!"
"This bird right here saved your life!"
"I know that! You don't have to rub it in!"
 Dayak stormed away.
"Humph!" Safra began to write:

Safra's Log
June 13th, 9:59 pm.

Today was another hectic day. Leopards chased us, the Captain revealed his name and a story, and I found a whistle, which summoned this peacock, which is both annoying and useful. The stars did a weird thing and protected us from the leopards!

I don't like Dayak (the peacock) very much, but I guess he's fine.

Safra

She closed it, and stared at the others, sitting around a fire. "I'll go join them," she murmured to herself.

She stuffed the notebook into her bag, and ran towards them. "What's for dinner, guys?" Safra asked.

"Chuck says he can make a vegetable soup!" Raisha licked her lips in anticipation.

"Yup," he said, "Chuck's vegetable soup is the drink of the sailors. Without it, we probably would not have survived!" the Captain joked.

"Yes, my soup is vital for survival," Chuck said, catching on. They all began to laugh, except Dayak.

"I hate soup," he said.

"How can you hate soup? Well, you can never hate Chuck's soup though," Ahmed said.

"I hate all kinds of soup," Dayak said. "Plus, it's hard for me to drink soup with a beak!"

"Oh, sorry," Ahmed said.

"Humph!"

"Oh, we're not wasting any good soup on a...*parrot*," the Captain sneered.

"I am not a parrot, and I don't want any soup!" Dayak's eyes narrowed.

"Then what are you, a chicken?"

"Arrrrgggghh!" Dayak jumped on top of the Captain and started to peck him with his beak.

"Get...Off...You woodpecker!"

"Woodpecker? You dare call me that? My feathers are skeleton keys! My beak is made of gold! My—"

"Yes, I do dare! Look at these white lies! No, literally! You're white in color, get it?!" The Captain laughed at his own joke, rolling on the ground.

"Dayak! Get ahold of yourself!" Raisha grabbed him by the neck again. "These are my friends, and you are not to hurt them. Understood?" she glared at him.

"Yes, understood, ma'am."

"Okay everyone, let's eat!" Raisha sat down in front of the fire, while the invisible Chuck made his soup. "Hey, Dayak," Safra called.

"What do you want, kid?" he frowned.

"Here's some fruit," she said. Safra had felt a little bad that he had saved their lives and now he wasn't being appreciated.

Dayak snatched them from her hand and walked away without saying a word.

"Of course," Safra rolled her eyes.

After dinner, all of them went into their tents. "Wow, that was tiring," Safra murmured, and fell into a deep sleep.

TWENTY-NINE

FIVE A.M. IN THE MORNING

Safra woke up to a scream.

She bolted outside and raced into Raisha's tent, where the sound had come from. "What happened? Did anyone die?" Ahmed had heard it as well. "No, it's just Dayak! Dayak, stop screaming!"

"But that sounded like it was a person!" Safra shouted. "My heart jumped into my throat!"

"Hearts can't do that!" Dayak said. "You're nuts."

"It's an EXPRESSION!" Safra was exasperated.

"Expression? As in a face expression?"

"NO!"

"Why are you getting so worked up?" Dayak really looked clueless.

Safra stormed away. "I'm going back to sleep," she muttered.

"No more sleeping! We have to get going! The Hunters could find us!" Raisha stopped her.

"Okay, fine," Safra groaned and began to help the others pack away all the tents.

"Let's get going!" the Captain said after all the packing.

Safra's eyes drooped. She checked her pocket watch. Five A.M.

"Can't we rest for a while before we begin?" Safra said, rubbing her eyes.

"No! We have to go! We can't be delayed because of a certain lazy person!" Raisha said.

"And why are you in such a hurry?" Safra snapped, insulted by her remark.

"Safra's not lazy! Don't call my sister that! We dragged you here with us!" Ridan exploded.

"Well, if I wasn't here, you all would not have known about the Hunters and you would have died!" Raisha snapped back.

"This is not about you saving us!" Ridan shouted.

"Then what is it about?"

"Raisha and Ridan! Stop it!" Ahmed shouted, pushing them back. "Raisha, you have no need to call Safra things like that. What time is it? It's five A.M. She would be tired."

Raisha hung her head, ashamed.

"And, Ridan! You don't have to snap at Raisha like that! Now you're putting yourself at fault as well," Ahmed said. "Now, Safra, if we are to return to camp soon, we must go now. Wash your face or something," the Captain said. "Let's go."

"Yeah," Safra yawned. "I'll try to stay awake," she said.

"Okay, then that's settled. But which way do we go?" Chuck asked.

"Towards the volcano, of course!" the Captain laughed. "We can't go any other way!"

"Of course. I forgot," Chuck yawned.

"He's so tired he can't even think straight!" Ridan said.

"Even me," he yawned too.

The Captain tried hard to suppress his yawns as well.

"Let's go. We can stop and make some breakfast somewhere else," he said.

Safra and Chuck both perked up at the mention of food.

"There we go!" Ahmed laughed heartily.

THIRTY

THE DARK FOREST

They walked out of the other side of the thicket. A straight path led to the volcano, which seemed even farther than ever. Safra felt like the volcano was moving away from them, although she knew that wasn't true. "Warm up your feet, everyone," Ahmed said. "This is going to be a long day."

Safra sighed. "I'm not going to last this one."

"Huh?" Ridan said.

"Nothing," Safra groaned.

They began to walk down the road, preparing for what they would face next.

The sky began to turn a light blue, signaling that it was morning. The birds chirped louder, and the sun became stronger. The cool, fragrant breeze wafted through the air.

"I think this might be a perfect place to make some breakfast. There's a forest over there, so we'll have a lot of kindling and fruit," Chuck said. "I'll make a berry cobbler or something like that."

"Yes, yes. Everyone go and gather some fruit and kindling! I'll stay with Chuck," the Captain said, and gave them containers to fill with fruit.

They went inside the thick, dense forest. It had an eerie feeling to it, as the tall trees did not let the sunlight pass through. Wilted, gray flowers littered the ground, covering the green grass.

"There are enough berries and kindling here. We don't have to go deeper," Ridan said.

"No, look at those juicy-looking ones over there. Going deeper isn't going to harm us," Safra said.

"I don't have a good feeling about this…" Ahmed agreed. "Of course not! Why are you so scared?" Raisha asked. "Let's go."

Dayak said, "I'll stay behind with…what's your name again?"

"My name is Ridan. And by the way, I am not staying back. You are coming with me."

"No! I thought you were staying…"

"Well no, I'm not."

Ridan dragged Dayak with him as he followed the others deeper into the forest.

"Oh no oh no oh no oh no," Dayak muttered. "I don't like this."

"Keep quiet, you little bird. Stop being such a…*Scaredybird*," Ahmed whispered.

"Why are you whispering?" Raisha asked.

"I feel like someone's following us. Never mind. I'm just a little nervous about this place."

"I know. Sometimes it feels like that when you're in a weird place, such as this," Safra admitted.

"But don't worry. There aren't any Hunters around here," Raisha said.

"You're still scaring me more," Ridan said, looking around nervously.

"Relax. There's a zero percent chance that they're going to be here." Raisha sighed.

"But what if they are here?" Safra asked.

"First brother, then sister. Do I have to spell it out for you? I told you, we're way ahead of the Hunters. They're never going to find us. Did you hear that? *Never*."

A bush rustled. The sound of a single twig cracking echoed through the air.

Safra quickly turned, but only to see Ahmed. "Sorry, that was me," he said sheepishly.

"I told you. There's nobody except us here," Raisha sighed. "You're such a bunch of fraidy-cats."

Safra seethed with anger. *What if a Hunter just suddenly ambushed us? Even Raisha would be scared. I'm just taking precautions. Bunch of fraidy-cats, huh? Whatever.*

Safra went back to picking. "Look, there are some wild strawberries!"

She also picked up some twigs in her free hand.

"Ooh, I love strawberries!" Ahmed knelt down to take a handful.

"This is going to be one awesome breakfast!" Ridan licked his lips.

"Mm," Safra filled her container with some blackberries. "Not too much strawberries. We should have a mixed variety," she mumbled.

As they carried the containers back to Chuck and the Captain, Safra looked over her shoulder, but only to see a black shadow in the depths of the forest.

She squinted, trying to make sense of the shape. It looked like a giant blob.

The bushes shook violently. She ignored it and walked away, clutching the kindling against her chest.

THIRTY-ONE

THE SHADOW

"Wow, Chuck, you're a great cook," Raisha said.
Everyone had just finished breakfast, and it was time to
get going again.
 "Let's move fast everyone," Ahmed said. "Come on!"
"Wait…We have to go inside that forest?" Ridan asked,
biting his nails.
 "Yes, of course! That's the way to the volcano!" the
Captain chuckled. Ridan sighed.
 "Oh, no!" Dayak screeched. "That forest gives me the
heebie-jeebies!"
 "We'll just go through it, that's all. There's nothing to
worry about."
 Oh brother, Safra thought.
 They walked into the forest, sidestepping large vines
and tree roots that looked like the just went on forever.
"Whoa!" Ridan tripped and fell.
Safra laughed and helped him get up. "You okay?" she
asked. "Yeah, I am," he said.

"Keep going! Safra, don't slow us down!" Raisha shouted
fiercely.

"Hey, he didn't fall on purpose!" Safra was getting tired
of Raisha's rants.

"Well, maybe he did!" she snapped.

"Well, why would I do that anyway?" Ridan stomped up
to her.

"Raisha! This is so childish! You're the one that's slowing
us down!" the Captain shouted. "Get back here, all of
you!"

They caught up with Chuck, the Captain, and Ahmed,
and Raisha muttered, "Sorry."

Safra pretended not to hear.

"Sorry," she said a little bit louder.

Safra nodded to acknowledge it. "Fine, then," she said.
But Ridan did not accept the apology. "Humph." He
walked ahead, ignoring her.

They kept walking throughout the thick trees and bushes.
Soon, they became used to the dim light.

"Shhhh. I hear something." Chuck stopped and turned
around.

"What? What did you hear?" Ahmed turned around as
well.

"I said 'shhhh'. I'm trying to listen," Chuck hissed.

"I don't hear anything," Raisha said.

"I said, SHHHH." Chuck turned his head to the left,
concentrating hard.

A dark shadow floated above their heads. Total darkness
swept over the forest.

"What is that?"

"I can't see anything!"

"It's so dark!"

"What?"

Everyone was talking at once, and they could only see faint outlines of each other. Safra looked up, only to see a dark platform above.

What is that? I can't see it very well.

She felt someone roughly grab her arm and drag her on the forest ground. It was a Hunter! They had even figured out how to trap Chuck by using a net.

"Let me go!" She struggled, but it was in vain. He held her in a viselike grip. He ascended a ladder and into the black platform, and then she realized that it was a building. Safra slipped the plaque beneath her shirt so that they wouldn't find it. Somehow, she knew it was important.

"It's a castle!" Ridan exclaimed.

"Shhhh!" the Hunter hissed.

"Wow," Safra whispered under her breath.

"Everyone, try to escape!" the Captain started to wiggle out of the Hunter's arms. "Let's get out of here!" he shouted. The rest of them copied his actions. The Hunter's grips were loosening. "It's working!" Safra yelled.

"They're showing resistance, my queen!" a Hunter shouted.

A silky, thick voice spoke, the sound reverberating through the room. "Do what you must do."

A powerful scent wafted through the air. Safra felt her eyes close, and everything turned black.

THIRTY-TWO

THE BLACK CASTLE

When Safra opened her eyes, she was in some kind of
dungeon. It reeked of fungus and rust. Their canteens
and food were all gone, plus their weapons and supplies.
 "My head," she groaned. A dizzy feeling crept over her.
 She looked around, only to see the others waking
up. *One, two, three, four, five… Six? Where's Raisha?*
 "Guys! Guys!" she tried to shake them awake.
 "Who—what?" Ahmed opened his eyes.
 "We're in a dungeon or something, and Raisha's gone!"
Safra shook him harder. "We need to find her!"
 "You—you—can—stop—shaking—me—me," he
stammered.
 "Oh, sorry," she let go of him. By this time, the rest of
them were awake.
 Safra repeated what she had just said, and Dayak started
to panic. "Oh no oh no oh no oh no oh no oh no oh no
oh no!" he started to pace the room, mumbling as he
went.
 "We're stuck here!" Ridan whined.

"No, we're stuck here…FOREVER!" Dayak was losing it.

"Dayak! Cool down! We'll find a way out of here!" Safra shouted. *What if we don't? What if we fail?* A voice in her head asked her. "And then we're going to die here, and we'll never have a happily ever after. Why? Why me?" Dayak went on and on.

"Dayak!"

His beak snapped closed, as if only noticing her now. "Ye—yes?" he stammered.

"Keep. Quiet." Safra clenched her teeth. "The last thing we need is negativity."

"You're right. We need to be positive," the Captain agreed.

"But what if we fail?" Safra whispered , nibbling on her fingernails. "Hey! I can hear someone!"

"SOMEBODY SAVE US!" Voices echoed through the hallway.

"My men!" the Captain shouted. "Shhhh. I can hear something else!"

The click-clacking of boots echoed in the hallway. "Our kidnapper is here. Stay cool," the Captain said, narrowing his eyes.

The slender woman in black armor stepped out in front of the bars of the dungeon.

The leader of the Hunters, Safra thought.

"Hello, my dear captives." Her voice was so sharp, with a slight lisp to it. Her silver staff clanged against the floor. Safra ran up to the bars. "Where is Raisha?"

"I have prepared some *zpecial* treatment for her," she laughed cruelly. Her blue and green eyes twinkled with a

mischievous glint. Her smile was perfect in every way, her
bouncy black curls cascading to her shoulders.

"By the way, Raisha deserves it," Ridan muttered.

"What have you done to her?" Ahmed asked.

"I just told you, I have been only *preparing* treatments for
her. I haven't done it yet!" She laughed again. "Don't you
know anything?"

Then, her voice took a more serious tone. "You messed
with the wrong person. Now, you will regret it, for sure."

"Let's see about that!" Ridan challenged. "Ridan!" Safra
shot him a warning look, but he pretended not to see it.

"Oh, and now a little five-year-old is threatening *me*?" her
eyes narrowed.

"I am not a five-year-old!"

"What are you going to do with us?" Chuck asked, trying
to be strong, but everyone could see that he was nervous.
Safra knew that all of them were scared.

"Take *zem* to the North Tower at midnight. There is no
way that *zey* will survive," she commanded her Hunters.
"You may go." She and her followers left the room.

"Now what are we going to do?" Dayak screeched. "Wait
until midnight, I guess," Safra sighed. Something was
waiting for them in the North Tower, and they did not
want to know what.

"Maybe…we should think of a plan," Chuck said.

"A plan? A PLAN?! Are you out of your mind! When do
you think we are going to escape this thing? Never, that's
when!" Dayak cried hysterically.

"Dayak! You've got to calm down! You're making
everyone else feel uncomfortable! I'm serious!" Safra
gritted her teeth. "If you could just stop, I would
appreciate it!"

An awkward silence filled the room.

"Humph! Fine then!" Dayak turned to face the wall.
"Dayak, Safra's right! Because of what you said, I'm kind of panicking too," Ahmed admitted.
Chuck said, "Me…Too."
"Humph," was the bird's only answer.
"Leave him. As I said, we need a plan," the Captain said.
"We have no chance of getting out of here. We just have to face what's coming," Ridan said.
"Yes. That is the only way."

THIRTY-THREE

THE NORTH TOWER

Safra woke to someone shaking her awake.

"It's midnight. Come."

Safra blinked. It was Ahmed. "They're going to take us to the North Tower." Safra rubbed her eyes and walked dizzily out of the dungeon and up some stairs, until they reached the top of the castle, on top of a tower. There was a wide hole in the middle of the floor. "Jump," the Hunter prodded.

Safra looked down. There was nothing but blackness. She kicked a pebble into it, and a tiny splash could be heard after a long time.

"Water!" Safra gasped.

"Jump!" the Hunter prodded again.

"What if I won't?" Ridan snapped.

He felt a sharp point touch his back.

"I'll jump! I'll jump! No problem. Heh heh," Ridan laughed nervously.

He stared at the deep, black emptiness that lay before him. He gulped.

"I'll go…First." the Captain stepped forward. "I am the Captain."

Sweat poured down his forehead. He closed his eyes.

"Captain…No," Safra whispered.

"It's time."

Was this it? Was this the end? Was this the end for all of them?

The Captain walked to the hole, and jumped.

Safra watched him until he became a small dot, and finally disappeared. She couldn't just wait there! She immediately jumped as well, yelling.

"CAAAPTAAINNNNNNNNNNNNNNNNNNNN!" She plummeted through the blackness, her body anticipating the cold water. It felt just like the time they had rescued Ahmed.

It felt like it was happening in slow motion. *Whenever I'm doing something fun, it seems to go by so fast. But it never is like that when something bad is happening, like…Falling to my death. It's going so slowly…*

She opened her eyes, and she remembered that she hadn't even said good bye to Ridan. What about her Grandpa? She looked up, and she could not see anyone else falling towards her.

It's probably only me and the Captain. Everyone else is going to live. Humph. At least I should have dragged Dayak along. Then the others could live in peace! Who am I kidding? She's going to kill them too!

She silently laughed, trying to reassure herself. She spread out her arms and legs, and stared upwards, towards the starry sky. Oh, how she wanted to fly high and touch those tiny twinkling stars! They looked so bright, like tiny lanterns.

She dared not look down. Although she knew that she was going to fall in it, she still did not have the courage. She was normally a very brave person, but this time…it was different. She knew she could never climb back up, and she would die for sure this time. She was going to be trapped there. *Forever trapped,* as Dayak would say.

Finally, she could see a figure falling towards her. It was Ridan, followed by the rest of them.

"RIDAN!" she tried to shout, but she could not talk underneath the water.

Safra was falling fast, and Ridan seemed to disappear. *Am I falling faster and faster?*

Then her whole body felt like it had been frozen. She immediately closed her eyes. *Brrrrr. This water is cold.* The water closed over her. But, she could still open her eyes. *Strange, again.*

She floated down, until she reached the bottom. She was running out of breath. Her lungs were burning, and she clenched her hands into fists. *Don't panic.*

She began to swim upwards, but her feet were rooted to the ground. *No. This can't be happening.*

She felt like she was being crushed by a large weight. *So this is how it feels to die.* A wave of fear washed over her. *Where is the Captain?*

A single fish swam through the water. *Come on, fish, give me your gills,* she thought.

She looked upwards, only to see Ridan plunging through the water.

He landed on the ground next to her. His face was all scrunched up.

Then, she had an idea.

She pointed to the fish. Ridan stared at her in confusion.

"Ridan! Talk to it!" she was screaming inside her mind. Come on, please understand.She tried to make motions with her hands.

Finally, he seemed to comprehend. He stared at the fish, and little bubbles came out of his mouth.

The fish started to grow bigger and bigger, until it became human size.

THIRTY-FOUR

FARO

Safra's eyes widened. She was just watching a fish grow in front of her eyes!

Then, the top of the fish just disappeared.

How?

It slowly started to materialize into the shape of a man's torso. The water began to turn and churn, and a merman was standing there. By this time Safra was completely out of breath. Her eyes started to close, but a blast of air hit her face. It was like living again!

A bubble now surrounded her and Ridan's heads. She could finally talk!

"Who are you?" Safra asked.

"I am Faro," he said, "I was imprisoned here years ago."

"Why did that Hunter lady do this to you?" Ridan asked.

"First of all, she is no 'Hunter lady.' She is a queen," he explained.

"Queen?"

"It's a long story. That's something you don't need to know. Anyways, what are you both doing here?"

"Actually, we're here with friends," Safra said, pointing to where the invisible Chuck, Ahmed and Dayak were floating. "Oh, and have you seen another man…" Ridan started. "Yes, I did. I have brought him to safety," Faro replied. *Phew, the Captain's safe,* Safra thought.

"You could take us to safety too," Ridan said.

"Will do," Faro said. After explaining to Chuck, Ahmed and Dayak, Faro led them through a tunnel, and as they were walking, Safra noticed something on the floor.

It was a locket, with an elephant obsidian stone inside it. She picked it up. It had blue stones, just like hers. *A Seer locket,* she thought. She turned it over, and there was a single word engraved in the stone.

'Meera.'

This was Meera's locket! But how had it gotten here? Safra stuffed it in her pocket. She would tell the others later. It was an important discovery!

I wish Raisha was here. She would know what to do with the locket… Safra sighed.

She noticed that the others had gone further ahead. "Wait for me!" she said, and ran after them.

As they exited the tunnel, her eyes met a wonderful sight. A beautiful house made by only stones and sand lay before her eyes. Beautiful coral surrounded it, complete with bubbly, colorful fish. Dolphins playfully chased each other, and turtles swam towards the surface.

"This took me a year to build," Faro explained. "What? You've been trapped here for a year?" Chuck gasped.

"Three years, actually. I figured I would be staying here for a long time, so I started to build a house for myself," he said.

"We're going to be stuck here for that long?" Chuck's voice seemed to shiver.

"There is one way out."

"Then why don't you try it?"

"Because it is too dangerous! I would rather live than try!" Faro said.

"What do we have to do to escape?" Safra asked.

"Oh no. Don't even think about it," Faro warned.

"It doesn't hurt to know," Safra said.

"Come inside," Faro said.

"Ah! My friends! Have you met my dear Faro?" the Captain raced to the doors with open arms. "Captain!" Safra hugged him.

"I was too, until he showed up!" the Captain laughed. "I owe you one, Faro," he said. "Don't mention it," Faro said.

"You are too modest, my friend," the Captain said and chuckled. "This is my most loyal part of my crew," he said, motioning to the rest of them.

"Oh. Please introduce yourselves."

Surprisingly, there was no water in the house. "It's so warm and dry," Safra said, smelling cinnamon.

After they had a nice chat, Faro asked, "I hope you don't mind if I ask, but, what is a young girl and boy doing on a dangerous adventure like this?"

"It's a long story," Safra chuckled. "That's the kind I like," he said.

"That's what everyone says!"

"Yes, yes. You must tell me anyways."

They talked and talked, until they lost track of time. "Oh, now I see," Faro nodded. "That's one adventure you've been having!"

"I know." Safra smiled.

"Well, back to reality." Chuck sighed. "We're never going to get out of here," he said sadly.

"Oh yes! By the way, Faro, you didn't tell me the way to get out of this place." Safra eyed him suspiciously.

Faro took a deep breath, hesitantly. "Okay. There is a huge pipe not far from here, and all you have to do is go up the pipe to the surface…"

"What, that's it?" Safra was surprised.

"No! Let me finish! A shark resides there. He will tear you up." Faro bowed his head. "And, plus, you need to lure the shark into a cage and trap it in there!"

"So you *did* go there?" the Captain asked.

"No…"

"Then how do you know about the sharks? Now I'm confused."

"I had a friend. He went inside, and you can imagine the rest." Faro did not seem to want to go in detail.

"Oh, Faro…" Safra did not know what else to say.

"That was two years ago, but I will never forget that moment," he said. His eyes filled with sadness.

"I understand. We must take leave of you," the Captain said. "But where will you go?" Faro asked.

"We are going to escape."

"How?"

"We will, somehow. Trust me. We have a special something we can use."

Faro did not seem to understand, but he gave them some supplies anyway. "I will stay here."

"You must come with us," Chuck said.

"That's okay. I shall stay here," he said. "As I told you, I would rather live."

"Thanks anyway Faro. You have saved our lives," they shook hands.
Faro watched them as they walked away into the clutches of death.

THIRTY-FIVE

ARNOLD

"Okay, Captain, what do you mean we have something special?" Safra asked.

"Your powers, of course! Ridan can talk to the shark, and you can use your visions to see what's ahead!"

"I can't just summon visions like that! We could use Chuck!"

"Just try."

She took a deep breath and closed her eyes.

My eyes adjusted to the darkness, and I looked upwards. A large gray shark swam around, patrolling the area. A cage hung in a corner. Everything fades away.

"The opening is clear, but there's a shark near the top. The cage is in the corner," Safra said. *Suprisingly, it worked!*

"All right Ridan, that's your cue," Ahmed said.

He nodded and swam into the pipe.

"Wait!" Safra said. "I'm not letting him go alone." She quickly swam after him.

Darkness covered them as they crouched down low into the pipe. Safra turned, but she could not see the rest of them. Her hands began to tremble as she spotted the shark above them.

"Whoa. That's huge," Ridan murmured.

"How are we going to lure it into the cage?" Safra murmured to herself. "I got it! We can use some food, like meat! Yes, yes, I'll distract it, you put in the meat—"

"I'm just going to talk to it," Ridan said and swam upwards, leaving Safra speechless.

"What? It's going to kill you!"

He ignored her warning and faced the shark. Bubbles came out of his mouth, and the shark seemed to respond.

Safra chewed on her fingernails. What if the shark suddenly attacked him? I'll stay calm, she told herself, but she could not.

"That's it! I'm going in there!" She followed Ridan's path.

"Ridan?" She looked around.

It was pitch black, and she could not see anything.

"Ridan?" She called again.

She closed her eyes, hoping for a vision, but nothing happened. "RIDAN!" Don't panic, she thought.

A powerful current of water swept over her. "Who is that? Show yourself!" She looked around. "Where's Ridan?!"

"It's me!" She squinted, and she could see an outline of Ridan— and a shark behind him!

"Ridan! The shark's behind you!" she shouted. "Don't worry. This is my friend, Arnold."

The shark flashed its teeth at Safra.

"He says hello, pleased to meet you," Ridan said.

"Ummm…Pleased to meet you too?"

"The Hunter queen imprisoned him and forced him to kill anyone who tries to escape. Arnold's pretty lonely, and I think I just became his friend," he said. "He said he's going to let us escape, because I told him I wouldn't put him in his cage! Bye, Arnold," Ridan said, and Safra waved to him. They told the others about what had happened.

"It's Ridan!" They all swam upwards. "Ridan! You did it, my boy!" Ahmed clapped him on the back. Safra hugged him. Chuck shouted, "Whoo! We've escaped!" and swam to the surface.

Safra swam next to him, and they all broke the water's surface.

The bubbles surrounding their heads popped and Safra took a deep breath, filling her lungs with the fresh air. They climbed out on the grass.

"Look! There's the castle!" They were near the rear of the building.

"Let's go. Crouch down!"

They crawled to a grassy spot, where they could not be seen. "Guys, I have to show you something!" Safra held out the locket she had found. The Captain took it, and studied the engraving. "That lady, huh? Hmmm."

"Yes. That Hunter queen looks just like her! Except that she has different colored hair and eyes," Safra said.

"I'm thinking that she has some sort of connection with all of this," Chuck said. "Yes, of course she would," Ahmed said.

"I wonder..."

"Well let's get going! We need to find the silver sand! We're so close, you see."

"But, Ahmed! What about Raisha?"

"Are you suggesting we go back there?"

"No, but..."

"We can't save Raisha. And without Raisha, we cannot complete her quest for her. It's her fault she wouldn't tell any of us about it."

"Ahmed has a point. We don't know anything about this." the Captain admitted.

Safra sighed. They were right.

"Where's Dayak?" Ridan asked.

"He's over there, eating…Fruit? Dayak! Come back here!"

"Oh right." He ran to them, his beak stuffed with food. "I was hungry," he said.

"What if we fail without Raisha? Whatever, let's go." Safra said, and took one last look at the castle. Ridan gave her a disapproving look.

"Stop talking about failing!"

Ignoring Ridan, she whispered, "I will save you, Raisha."

THIRTY-SIX

GUILT STRIKES

Safra was still worried about Raisha. What would become of her?

She's probably imprisoned.

She hung her head. She could not think about the silver sand, only about Raisha. "Why? Why? Why did we ever take Raisha with us? Now look!" Safra scolded herself.

"What are you talking about? I can't hear you!" Dayak said.

"I'm not talking to you. I'm talking to myself," she said.

"Well, what were you saying?"

"That's none of your business, you silly bird!"

"Well, that's rude! Where's Raisha? When are we going to save her?"

"I honestly don't know," Safra said.

Dayak didn't continue the conversation after that. An eerie silence followed.

"Dayak?"

"Mm?"

"I'm sorry. You know, for saying that."
"Apology accepted."
"Fine."
"Fine."
Another silence sliced the air.
"Come on! Let's keep going!" the Captain said, trying to see if anyone would start a conversation, but no one said anything. It was obvious that they all were guilty that they were leaving Raisha behind.
"Can't we…Go back?" Chuck asked slowly.
"No! Of course not! We can't let that queen know that we're alive!" Ahmed said.
"But we know how to escape from the North Tower," Chuck insisted.
"If she knows we're alive, she won't put us back in the North Tower!" Ridan said.
"Duh," Safra said.
"So, we just keep walking."
"Yes."
No one said anything for a while. Safra had never felt this bad in her entire life.
Why did Raisha have to come along? Now, all I feel is guilt.
"Too bad we had to leave Raisha behind," Chuck sighed. "I feel really bad." The rest of them nodded.
"Umm…Excuse me? Do you think we're going to go back there?" Ridan rolled his eyes.
"But…"
"Would you?"
"No…But…"
"Exactly my point. Let's just forget about it."
"Ridan!"
"What?! We all feel guilty. But, we all know that we can't do anything as well! Now, let's forget about it, and go on with our own quest!"

Safra remained silent. *So, this is it. I'm never going to find out
about Meera, or what secrets Raisha was exactly talking about.
I will solve this mystery, even if it's the last thing I do.*
Safra stared at the castle. She could hear a voice shouting,
"Help! Help!"
She was imagining it, wasn't she? Was it real? She glanced
at the others, who did not look back.
Of course they hadn't heard it. "Guys, wait up!" She
raced to catch up.
"Guys! Did you hear that?" she asked.
"No, what?" Ridan looked back at her.
"Nothing," she said.
But, as she looked back, she was sure that she could see a
silhouette of a girl, standing at the bars of a window, her
hair flapping in the wind.

THIRTY-SEVEN

SAFRA'S PROMISE

"I didn't realize that we were so close to the Mona!" the Captain exclaimed.

Wait. What about the Silver Dawn Legend? What is it?

"I think the Hunters' castle moved! We're not near the forest anymore!" Safra realized.

"A simple stroke of luck!" Ahmed smiled.

"No more obstacles! Nothing but the sand!" the Captain jumped for joy. "It's my dream come true!"

Safra smiled and looked at Ridan. She had never seen the Captain this happy.

"I'm happy if you're happy, Henry," Ahmed said, and the two friends began to sing some old sea ballads.

"Ah, this is the life," the Captain said. "I love going back to being old friends."

"Yep," Ahmed nodded.

Chuck's voice was bright and happy. "I'm so happy to see that these two are best friends again."

"I agree," Safra said.

"I like this Captain better," Ridan said. "The funny, awesome Captain is…Well…Awesome!"

"Yep. Now we're going to get the sand, and we can see if the legend is true!" Chuck agreed.

"You mean you don't know if the legend is true?"

"Yes, we do, but it still could be a rumor," Chuck said. "I mean, all the evacuees claim it, so it's probably true. They say that the rulers use it only when they have a crisis."

"Rulers? Who were the rulers?"

"I don't know," Chuck said.

"Hmmm…I wonder if…"

"Wonder what?"

"Oh, nothing. It was just a thought." Safra said.

"Well, I don't know why they didn't use the silver sand to escape either…I mean this is all so confusing! Ugh," Chuck muttered.

"Yeah, I know, right? I just want to get this over with, so I can go home and just be normal again."

"What? I thought you didn't want that."

"Not anymore. I've had enough," Safra said.

"That doesn't sound like the Safra I know," Chuck said. "Come on."

"Yeah, I know. I didn't really mean that, I'm just tired. Well, I'm part of the crew! I will go on more adventures. If I stay home for too long, I'll probably be bored." Safra said. "I guess I kind of live on adventure." "That's the way to go!" Chuck smiled.

"Yeah, I couldn't imagine my life without it." Safra smiled back.

"Well, I still hope the Hunters don't come after us again," Chuck said. "That's one thing I don't want," he shivered.

"Well, she got Raisha so…" Safra's heart sank.

"Yeah…I still wish we could go back. And…" Chuck's voice cracked.

"I feel like we betrayed her!" Safra burst out in tears. "She was such a good friend, and now we're just leaving her there!"

"Safra…"

"Well, whatever." Safra said. "I shouldn't be thinking about that." She dried her face with a handkerchief.

"That's better. Come. Let's go," Chuck walked with her. *What have I become? I'm actually leaving a friend behind. No, this is not me. I shouldn't be leaving her behind. Should I ask the Captain? No, he was right. We can't save her. Ahmed says it's dangerous, which it is. The Captain agrees. Why can't we just try? Well, I guess that's just the way it goes. Wait…what about the Captain's men?*

Safra decided that, after her adventure was over, she would come back to the castle with reinforcements, and save Raisha— if she was still there. Maybe she would be on time, because they were closer to the Mona than expected. Those thoughts made her feel better.

Safra had made her promise— and she wouldn't break it.

THIRTY-EIGHT

ON THEIR TRAIL

As they walked on, the Mona started to look closer and closer. "Wow! We're so close!" Ridan exclaimed.

"So close, and yet so far. I mean, what if we face certain dangers in the volcano? There's bound to be traps." Ahmed sighed.

"This is going to be harder than we expect." Ridan muttered.

"Look on the bright side of things! The Hunters won't come and ambush us again!" the Captain said.

"They might, if we're discovered," Chuck said. "What if the queen found out that we were alive?"

"Nah, she'll never know. She's not going to go and check if we're dead or not," Ahmed said. "We're free from the Hunters for good!"

"I'm still not so sure," Chuck said.

"Oh, Chuck. Stop jumping to conclusions!" Ahmed sighed and laughed.

"Let's take a small rest," the Captain said. "I'm exhausted from all that swimming. My ears are clogged!"

Safra plopped down on the ground, too tired to think.
Her eyes closed, and she fell into a gentle sleep.

*I close my eyes, only to appear in the Hunter queen's castle. I am
standing on a balcony, and she is standing only a few feet away from
me.*

A Hunter rushes to her side.

"My queen, you are right," he gushed. "They have escaped!"

*"Hmmm...Faro has helped them. I must punish him for that.
Track them down! Find them, and bring them to me! I don't care if
you even kill some. But the question is: how did they outsmart the
shark?" Her eyes narrowed. "Go! Take your troops with you! I
will come."*

*"Yes, ma'am," he saluted and rushed out of the room. I could see
Hunters descending to the ground, and they took off on their horses
immediately, heading towards the path we had took, and the queen
joined them. Blackness covered my eyes.*

"No!" Safra jolted upright.

"What?" the Captain looked at her.

"A vision...the Hunters are after us!" Safra gasped. Her
visions were getting weirder and weirder. They
were...different. It wasn't the future, it was happening as
they spoke!

She was seeing the present, but in a different place! It
was like she was in two places at once. *This might be useful.*

"WHAT?!" Ahmed was shocked. "No! We need to keep
moving!"

"Yes...If what Safra says is true, then we must keep
moving, and we must move fast. No time for breaks."

"Yes! It's true! Really!" Safra insisted.

Ridan gave her a look. Safra pretended that she didn't see
it, and got up.

"Let's go."

"Yes, let's go."

"I hope the Hunters won't catch us anytime soon." Chuck shivered.

"Me too," Ahmed said.

They began to walk down the path, hoping for the best of things.

THIRTY–NINE

THE COTTAGE

They had walked a long way. Safra's legs ached, making it harder to walk. A bubbling stream ran beside them. "Captain, look at that!" Ridan pointed to a fork in the road.

 "Yes, there are two paths. What about that?"

 "No, look at that! There's a cottage in the middle of the paths! If people live there, maybe they'll know a shortcut or something," Ridan said. "These people could save our lives!"

 "I get it Ridan. Yes, yes, there is a good chance one of these paths could be a shortcut."

 "Then let's go!" Ahmed walked up and knocked on the door. A middle-aged woman opened it.

 She looked very elegant and well-dressed. A fur coat was wrapped around her, and shining jewelry adorned her neck. Her smooth blonde hair flowed freely down her back.

 "Janina! Ellie! We have visitors!" she called sweetly. "Come in, come in."

Two other women, who looked very much like the first
one, appeared in the doorway. "Oh, we have visitors!
Visitors! How nice!" they cooed. "Come in, come in."
Safra stepped inside of their house, but looked much
bigger than what it had looked from the outside. "How
is that happening?" Safra muttered.

"Oh, those are just mirrors, dear. They make the house
bigger and more welcoming," the first lady said. *Whoa!
Those must be some sharp ears!*

"Yes, yes, of course it will," Safra nodded. She turned to
face the wall. *No. Wait. That's the mirror. I can see myself!*
It had been such a long time since she had looked at
herself. Her already tanned skin had become darker, and
her black hair was now matted. She had never cared
much about her appearance back at home. But now she
yearned to be clean— and pretty.

She brushed her greasy hair out of her face. Her clothes
were shabby and torn. She sighed, staring at herself. "Let
me introduce myself. I am Dulcie, and this is Janina and
Ellie." The woman who had opened the door spoke.

"Ahmed. This is Henry, Safra, Ridan, and Dayak."

They left Chuck out of it, because he was, of course,
invisible.

"Charmed," Dulcie said, holding out her hand, and
shook hands with each of them.

"Oh, dear, let's get you all cleaned up," Ellie rose from
her seat. "Safra, am I right? You can come with me." She
had spoken as if she had read Safra's mind. She followed
Ellie into another room.

She allowed Safra to take a bath, and combed out her
hair until it was all shiny and glossy. A thick, light blue
shirt hung loosely around her shoulders.

"There!" Ellie adjusted the small earrings that Safra was
wearing. "It's done!"

Safra set her rucksack on the floor, and turned to look at herself. The turquoise studs stood firmly in her ears, and her hair was now was flowing and carefree.

"Thanks…Ellie. I really mean it."

"Oh, don't mention it dear," she said. "You look absolutely stunning!"

Safra smiled. She stepped out of the room. "How do I look?" she asked.

Ahmed started to laugh. Ridan put his hand over his mouth.

"What are you laughing at?" Safra's face reddened.

"Headlines! Headlines! Safra the Brave is wearing earrings!" Ahmed fell out of his chair, guffawing and snorting.

"What's the matter with my earrings?"

"You look so funny! You almost never wear earrings!" Ridan couldn't hold his laughter back either.

"Don't say that! Don't you want to get cleaned up yourself? " the Captain warned.

"Stop making fun of Safra like that!" Chuck muttered, making sure the ladies could not hear him.

Safra felt anger rising up inside her. She gritted her teeth. "Both of you stop acting like inconsiderate fools!"

Ahmed looked up to see Dayak standing above him.

"What did you just call me?" Ahmed's face twisted into a frown.

"I called you an inconsiderate fool!" Dayak fumed.

Ahmed grabbed him by the neck. "How dare you call me that?!"

"I can call you that if I want!"

"Oh yeah?"

"Yeah!"

"Both of you stop it!" Safra said. "Yes, maybe I look funny, then, forget it! Ahmed, let go of Dayak!" she commanded. He slowly let go of his neck.

By this time, Ellie, Janina and Dulcie had stood up. "How dare you insult a girl like that!" they chorused. Ridan looked down at his feet, avoiding Safra's gaze. She remained silent.

Dulcie disappeared into another room. She looked carefully around the room, to see if anyone else was watching.

Hmmm. Suspicious, Safra thought. While the other ladies where scolding Ahmed and Ridan, Safra tiptoed down to the room where Dulcie had went into.

"Yes, as you said. They're here. Yes, yes, they may leave. Come quickly!" she was whispering to herself as she wrote something on a piece of paper. She walked over to a cage that held a pigeon, and attached the paper to its leg.

A letter! Of course! Dulcie released the pigeon out of its cage, and it flew gracefully out of the window.

"That will be enough. We shall be rewarded," she muttered, looking out the window. She slowly turned towards Safra's direction.

She quickly ducked behind a wall, and instinctively reached for her rucksack.

Oh no! It's in the other room! My bow and arrows! She heard Dulcie walking out of the room, and dashed away.

FORTY

SUSPICIOUS

"Guys!" Safra shouted.

She had sprinted into the room and grabbed her rucksack.

"What?" the Captain asked her.

"I…I saw a creature outside! Grab your weapons!" she lied. She did not want to accuse the ladies. *Safra, calm down,* she told herself. *What if they're innocent?*

The Captain's hand went to the hilt of his sword. "A creature?"

CRASH! BOOM! The door flew open.

Safra whirled around. The shadows of Hunters filled the room.

"Hunters!" Ridan shouted. The Captain drew his sword. Ahmed grabbed his.

"Escape!" Safra pointed to the back door. The Hunters, hearing this, turned. At that second, Safra grabbed Ridan by the arm and dragged him out of the front door.

"Everyone, come out!" Safra shouted. The Hunters followed them outside as well.

"Run!" Chuck shouted.

"No! Hide! Remember what Raisha told us?" Ridan yelled. He ducked underneath a bush.

"Ridan's right!" Safra climbed a tree and hid herself behind the leaves.

Ahmed jumped into the stream that was near the path. Bubbles surfaced in the spot where he had jumped. The Captain jumped alongside him.

Chuck snuck into the action, waiting to launch a surprise attack, and meanwhile, Dayak had dashed behind a rock.

The Hunters paced around in circles, waiting for them to come out. One of them stood right beside the tree Safra was hiding in.

Safra steadied her bow. *Aim— and…Fire!*

The arrow threw him off his horse. Safra jumped from the tree and onto its back.

Riding a horse is hard. I wonder how they ride and shoot arrows! She awkwardly held the reins, unsure of how to use them. She decided to copy the other Hunters' movements.

"Hyah!" she squeezed her feet together and leaned forward, and suddenly the horse took off at full speed. As she rode past the fallen Hunter, she bent down and stole his silky black cloak. Still holding the reins with one hand, she wrapped it around herself. "There! Now I'm a Hunter!" she whispered to herself and chuckled. "Ah!" She could hear Ahmed's scream.

He had jumped out of the stream, and he was outnumbered. Three Hunters swarmed around him, holding sharp knives and swords.

I'll go and help him, she thought, and leaned to the left. The horse cooperated, and she steered herself towards him.

Ahmed, not knowing who she was, took a swipe at her
with his sword. She backed away.

"It's me," she hissed.

"Safra?" he stopped fighting for a second.

"Look out!" she whispered.

He turned around just in time to block another Hunter.
They had not noticed Safra.

She made sure all the other Hunters were not looking in
their direction. Then, with a swift motion, she whipped
out her bow and arrow. She fired three of them, which hit
their targets perfectly.

"Th—thanks," Ahmed stammered, embarrassed. Safra
turned around without saying another word. She adjusted
her cloak, and rode towards the others, who had also
started fighting.

"Safra…"

She did not turn around.

"Hyah!" She urged her horse to go faster. "Ridan!
Chuck! Dayak! Captain! Ahmed. It's just me! Listen to
me. Go and hide!"

"Safra?"

"Hide!"

They disappeared behind some bushes. Safra turned to
face the Hunters.

"They jumped in a river!" she said in a deep, dry voice.
They looked at her doubtfully.

Safra followed them, but slipped away at the last
moment.

She watched them ride away, and once they were out of
sight, she whispered, "Guys? Are you still there?"

They emerged out of the bushes. "Safra, that was brilliant!" the Captain said. "We now have a fine horse as well!"

She smiled. "Now we're finally rid of those Hunters," she said.

Ridan and Ahmed looked quite ashamed of themselves. "Thank you." Ahmed said.

"No mention," Safra said dryly.

Ahmed hung his head. "Well, I guess we go to the Mona now," Chuck said.

"Yes, we shall finally reach the volcano." The Captain wiped sweat off of his forehead.

Safra sighed. "Isn't anyone tired after that fight?"

But nobody seemed to listen to what she was saying.

That's the way it goes.

FORTY-ONE

FINALLY

Sounds of birds chirping filled the air.

"There's the Mona!" the Captain pointed.

"I guess we chose the right path," Chuck said. Large blue birds flew in a 'V' across the sky.

"They're beautiful," Safra said.

"Yes! It's magnificent!" the Captain agreed.

"I wish I could fly like that," Safra said.

Unusually, Ahmed and Ridan were very quiet. She noticed it. "Ridan, what do you think we should name this horse?" she asked.

"Huh?"

"What do you think we name this horse?" she asked, grinning.

"How about we call him Khan?"

"Khan! That seems fine," Safra said. "That's a fitting name for a majestic horse like him, because means *great ruler.*" The Captain smiled. "Yes, yes. We shall let him carry our rucksacks."

They placed their supplies on his back, and Safra held the reins, to make sure that he wouldn't run away.

"His coat is really shiny," she said, digging her fingers into its soft mane. Khan whinnied appreciatively.

"Come, let's go on," Ahmed said, avoiding Safra. "Wait. What if we all ride the horse? We can get there faster!" Safra suggested.

"But all of us can't fit!" the Captain said.

"We could build a back cart or something," Safra said. "We could use some of those logs over there too."

"Hmm. Seems like a plan," Ridan said. They got to work, and after a few tries, they finally got it right.

"All aboard!" Ridan yelled out. The Captain took the reins, and the rest were in the cart.

"Hyah!" The Captain leaned forwards, and Khan took off on full speed.

The Captain was a pretty experienced horse rider. He easily maneuvered around the steep curves, avoiding rocks and little pits on the path.

"I like the idea of using this cart," Ridan said. "Good idea…Safra."

She didn't say anything back. "Safra?" Ahmed said. "What?"

"I'm sorry for making fun of you." He nudged Ridan. "I'm sorry too," Ridan said.

Before Safra could reply, the Captain shouted, "There it is!" The Captain yelled. "The Mona!"

Beautiful, lush green trees surrounded the towering volcano. "I guess it's dormant, right?" Chuck asked doubtfully.

"I don't know, actually," the Captain admitted.

"But what of it erupts?" Dayak started to imagine the worst scenarios that could happen.

"Dayak! Don't panic already! It won't erupt, at least not now. Maybe." the Captain didn't look so sure of himself either.

Dayak shivered. "But what if…"

"Dayak! No *what ifs!* Just remember, *stay positive*," Safra said.

"Okay. Stay positive," Dayak repeated.

"Take a deep breath," she instructed.

Dayak obeyed.

"Now do this every time you panic."

"Okay."

Safra smiled. A wave of happiness washed over her. They were finally here, but without Raisha.

She couldn't be satisfied with herself unless she solved the Meera mystery and saved Raisha. "What do you think could have happened to her?" she thought out loud.

"Happened to whom?" Chuck asked.

"Raisha," she answered.

"I don't know Safra. It's best not to think about her." Chuck said. He obviously didn't want to talk about it.

"But I feel guilty!" Safra said. "We have to rescue her!"

"Safra… We can't do anything about it anymore," Ahmed said. "It's not anyone's fault, either."

"I know that! But I feel like we've made a mistake," Safra sniffled.

"We are going back to save her…right?" Dayak asked.

Safra shook her head, tears cascading down her face. She opened her mouth, but no sound came out. She hugged Dayak to her chest.

"My master is gone!" he squawked.

Safra sighed. Crying was useless. Why was she crying anyways? *I'm not going to be weak. I even promised to myself that I will save her.*

 But she knew that, deep down, it would probably be impossible to keep the promise.

FORTY-TWO

DREAMS COME TRUE

They reached the mouth of the Mona. "We're here." the Captain dismounted the horse and fell to his knees. "My lifelong dream has come true!" His happy tears dripped onto the ground.

Safra smiled. Today was their day. They had reached their goal. *Mom and Dad, hope you're proud of me.* She closed her eyes, smiling.

All of their work had finally paid off.

Ahmed walked over to the Captain. "I'm so happy for you, Henry," he said.

"I couldn't have done it without you," he said, and they shook hands and embraced each other.

Chuck ran to them. "Come on everyone! Group hug!"

"Oh no," the Captain said, but it was too late. He and Ahmed were caught in Chuck's heart-wrenching hug. It looked rather peculiar, as they could not see Chuck, only his jacket.

Safra, Ridan and Dayak decided to stay out of it. "I would probably be crushed by now," Ridan said. "I would probably die, because of this thin neck of mine." Dayak cleared his throat.

Safra chuckled. "I'm not a fan of group hugs," she said and smiled.

The Captain and Ahmed had finally managed to escape Chuck. Sweating and panting, they plopped down on the ground next to Ridan. "Take me away from Chuck!" Ahmed pleaded.

Safra, Ridan, and Dayak started to laugh.

"Why are you running away from me?" Chuck said. Safra chuckled. She knew that he already knew the answer to his own question.

"Eh…" the Captain looked at Ahmed.

"It's okay fellas, I know why you're running away from me, I'm only joking," Chuck clapped Ahmed on the back.

"Heh heh. Very funny." Ahmed narrowed his eyes. "We still have to cure you, Chuck," he said.

"Well, let's go inside the Mona!" the Captain said. "You do the honors, Captain," Safra said.

"No, Safra. It was because of you I learned something. I learned to have courage, and you inspired me," he said. "I want you to do it."

"But…"

"No buts. Do it," he said, and smiled.

Safra knew it was hard for him to do that because it was his dream. But then, she realized, it was hers too. She took a deep breath, and stepped inside of the mouth of the Mona.

She had expected a certain image in her mind, but, there was nothing. There was a stone ceiling above her, and a man stood guard next to a door. "I'm not inside the Mona yet. There's a door and a man! Guys! You better come here!"

They rushed inside. "Is anything wrong?" Chuck asked. "Kind of…"

"He looks like a statue," Ahmed whispered.

The man's facial expression did not change. He did not move a single muscle. Not even his mustache moved. Safra walked up to him and waved her hand in his face. "He isn't moving," she whispered, turned away from him. Then, she felt a sharp point touch her back. She whirled around to see that the guard had moved. He was small and very round, but his mustache was so huge it covered his mouth!

"Umm…I'm here in peace!" Safra said.

"Why are you here?" his mustache bobbed up and down as he spoke.

"I'm here to uh…Here to…Uh…Um."

"I want the answer to my question."

She looked at the Captain. He nodded.

"I'm here for the silver sand," she said firmly.

"No! You may not enter."

"Why not?"

"I, The Guardian of The Silver Sand, am not permitted to let anybody inside."

Then Dayak walked up to the Guardian and whispered something to him. He nodded, and said, "I shall break the news to you. You cannot open this door." "Why not?" Ahmed asked.

"The key is with the queen," the Guardian explained.

"What queen?" Safra asked.

"So you do not know?" he looked surprised.

"I never knew where the key was— anyways, they are new to our world, Guardian," Dayak said. "I have not told them the story, but I guess there is a time for everything to be revealed." Dayak sighed. "Tell them," he said.

FORTY-THREE

LEGEND OF THE SILVER DAWN

The Guardian cleared his throat. "It all began about twenty years ago, when Silver Island flourished, and we had a king and queen. But one day, they abdicated the throne, and handed over the crowns to their thirteen-year-old daughters on their birthday. They earned their lockets, and…"

"Explain to me about these lockets," Safra said.

"Well, whenever a person from the royal family becomes thirteen, they are given magical lockets. These lockets determine their powers. They can become either a Seer, Healer, or a Whisperer, and they are supposed to wear it all the time. It is a sign of their origin, and, if they lose it and somebody else wears it, the power will go to the person who is currently wearing the locket," he said.

"How are these lockets created?" Safra asked.

"They are created by a powerful object called the Rose Scepter," he replied.

This is all beginning to make sense, Safra thought, remembering the Scepter from her vision.

"Moving on," he said. "The two daughters were given half of the kingdom each. They ruled in peace, until…" he faltered.

"Go on," Safra urged.

"The Rose Scepter has two parts. There is a silver staff, and a head for it that is shaped like a rose. It is made of pure silver, and the two daughters were given half of the Rose Scepter each as well," he said.

"Well, what does that have to do with the story?" Safra prodded.

"Patience, my child," he said. "Then…"

"Wait… What were the names of the two queens?" the Captain asked.

"Neera and Meera," the Guardian answered. "Now stop interrupting me!"

Wait. So the Hunter queen that looks like Meera is Neera? Safra was becoming very excited on learning this piece of news.

"Well, moving on. One day, Neera asked for the other half of the Rose Scepter, and did not tell Meera why she wanted it. Meera refused, and they got into a fight. Meera gave it to her in the end, but told Neera she had to return it when she asked for it. But she was not aware of Neera's motives. Neera planned to create many, many more lockets so she could have more power. You see, she was jealous that Meera was a powerful Seer, and Meera was also taught by a teacher to make her powers stronger. Neera chose to learn sword-fighting because she had the mere power of a Healer, and it takes time for a Healer's powers to develop, but it is not the case for Seers. They

develop their powers quite quickly, and have a wonderful
memory. Neera also wanted to experiment and create
new powers, instead of the same old ones." He paused
and took a deep breath.

"But Neera always tried to make a Seer locket. She
mainly wanted to be a more powerful Seer than Meera.
The problem was that Seer lockets are very rare. But one
day, Neera succeeded, after many tries. And, by that time,
Meera had found out about what she was up to, and she
immediately threw away all the lockets. Neera had created
so many, they littered the kingdom. People found it and
kept it for themselves." *Was this how Safra had gotten her
locket?*

He continued. "Neera was outraged. The Seer locket was
gone, and she was so angry that she stole Meera's locket.
It backfired a little, as she wore both lockets at once, hers
and Meera's. That is why she has two different colored
eyes. One is the power of the Healers, and the other of
the Seers. Luckily, Meera was able to take away the locket,
and she never trusted Neera again."

"Later on, when they were older, more people started to
live on Silver Island, and there were a lot of debates on
whether to use the silver sand or not. Everyone knew that
there were consequences, but Neera did not believe it.
She started to use it, and began to rely heavily on it.
Meera didn't like this, and she threatened to lock away all
the silver sand into this very volcano and keep the key."
"Neera did not believe in it and ignored the warnings, but
soon, the consequences became real. The island was hit
with storms and hurricanes. Meera blamed Neera, and
took away the sand. Neera, in rage, cursed her with the
one locket she still kept." he paused again to catch his
breath.

"She cursed her, to disappear forever, on the day of the full moon. That day, dawn never came and the night lasted throughout the day, but the sky filled with silver streaks and shooting stars! It was called the Silver Dawn. Year after year, the Silver Dawn came and went. That was the only time that Meera's curse could be broken. But no one tried. Since then, Neera spelled the island, and it was hidden from sight. She didn't want anyone to return, because Meera was gone and she did not know what to do."

"What do we have to do to break the curse?" Safra asked.

"Meera lost her locket before she was cursed because of Neera, who threw it away. If she wears her locket, she can break out of it," the Guardian explained.

"So the key to the silver sand is with Meera now?" Ahmed asked.

"Yes." he nodded.

"When is the next Silver Dawn?" Safra asked.

"Tomorrow," the Guardian said.

"Tomorrow?! We can't do this!" the Captain's hat fell off his head.

"So if we don't break this Meera's curse, we can't open this door to the sand?" Ahmed asked.

"I'm afraid not," the Guardian said, his mustache drooping.

"But...We have to break this curse if we want our sand? No—no!" the Captain fell to the ground.

Safra was blown away. They had come here for nothing. Then she realized that Meera was also their only hope for Chuck to be cured.

"Dayak, you didn't tell us about this!" Ridan exploded. "Now, we've lost everything!"

"I never knew about the key! I thought the Guardian had the key or something! Leave me alone!" he pleaded.

"Now what?" Ridan looked at Safra. She sighed. "I don't know."

FORTY-FOUR

DESPERATE

"So…where exactly is Meera now?" Ahmed asked. "No one knows," the Guardian said. "I know what you're thinking— if no one knows where she is, no one can restore her locket to her either."
 We have the locket, but we don't have Meera…" Safra murmured.
 "This is impossible! We don't even know where she is!" Ahmed slumped to the ground. The Captain sighed.
 "Wait…Guardian?"
 "Yes?"
 "How did the people know about these consequences?" she asked, although she could already guess the answer. "There was a stone plaque that was found years ago. It remains in the Silver Serpent Cove, and it had a poem that explained everything. Meera believed it, Neera didn't."
 "Well, it doesn't remain in the Cove any longer!" Safra said, whipping out the plaque from her bag.

"The plaque!" the Guardian's eyes widened in surprise.
"Yes," Safra said.
The Captain got up. "Why didn't we use this?"
Safra sighed.
"Ridan didn't believe it. He thought it was a fake," Safra said. "We found it at the Cove, and there was a drawing of Meera…" Safra trailed off in thought. "Her hands felt real…I got it!" she jumped in joy.
"Wait…I think I get it too," Ridan said slowly. "Meera was imprisoned within the Cove!" Safra exclaimed.
"Yes!" Ridan said.
"Wait. I don't get it," Ahmed said.
"There was a drawing of Meera I had to touch if I should get the map and the plaque," Safra said, "and when I did touch it, her hand felt real, like skin! She even had a bracelet with a key!" Safra said. "Wow," Ahmed breathed.
"The Guardian spoke up. "You mean you know where Meera is?"
"I think so. It's just a theory," Safra said, "but it'll be really hard to get there."
"Oh, that's a problem." the Captain scratched his head.
"What if we tried?" Safra asked. "I mean, it might be possible."
"We can't go all the way back!" Chuck's jacket jumped up and down.
"We have Khan. We could try, you know. Would you rather do that or wait for another year to find the sand?" Safra raised an eyebrow.
"I guess it's worth it," Chuck said.
"Yes. It seems reasonable," Ahmed said.
The Captain frowned.

They stared at him, putting their hands together, giving him hopeful looks.

He smiled and nodded.

Ahmed walked up to the Guardian. "Don't be relaxed. We won't be gone for long," he said, staring hard into the Guardian's eyes.

"Um— ok," he stammered, surprised by Ahmed's sudden warning.

Ahmed nodded sharply, turned, and went over to join the rest of them.

"We have no time to lose," the Captain said. "Let's get on with this!"

"Yeah!" Safra raised her fist.

"EEYAH!" Ridan shouted out their war cry.

"EEYAH!" Safra repeated.

"EEYAH!" Ahmed and Chuck shouted at the top of their lungs.

The Captain chuckled, but gave in. "EEYAH EEYAH!" he raised his head up to the sky and shouted.

Safra smiled, and threw her bag into the cart. "Let's go!"

FORTY-FIVE

A PROBLEM ARISES

The Captain mounted Khan, and they were off. He urged the horse to go faster and faster.

"Give the horse a little break, Captain," Safra chuckled.

"I can hear Khan panting," Ridan said.

"I'm the rider, okay? I'm trying to make sure that I'm going on the right path," the Captain grunted.

"I'll take over," Ahmed said.

"That's fine, Ahmed. I'll hand it over later. After all, we've just started," the Captain said.

Safra was in worry. It was already getting a little dark. *How in the world will we reach the coast in a few hours? Maybe, if we do, we could swim to the Cove. But that's too long. What if we fail?*

She sighed.

"Wait. We didn't think of one thing," Safra said.

"What now?" Dayak drooped.

"Remember when I lied to the Hunters? They would have figured it out by now! They would be coming for us! They're heading towards us right now! If we keep going like this, they'll ambush us!" she said. "We need a shortcut."

"We don't know any shortcuts. Face it, we have to fight them," the Captain said, his hand flying to the hilt of his sword. "Keep your arms at the ready!"

As Safra took out her bow and arrows, she said, "But Captain, they'll slow us down. We can't possibly get to the coast in time!"

He didn't answer. After a few moments of silence, he said, "I think we should try."

The sound of horse hooves clopping against the ground filled the air. Safra knew what it meant. The Hunters had arrived.

"Just like Safra predicted," Ridan said. "They're here!" The Captain and Ahmed unsheathed their swords. "We must be prepared this time. Confuse them. We must hide, and then we attack if they are close to finding us," the Captain said. "At this signal," he said, flicking his hand in a smooth movement, "everyone come to fight. Remember to give this signal if you are in danger." he jumped into a bush. "Hide!"

They hid themselves from view, including Khan. "Where did they go? I thought I saw them," a Hunter blurted out.

"Yes, yes," they mumbled to themselves. One Hunter whispered something into another's ear.

Safra strained her ear to hear what they were saying, but she could not.

Stay still, she told herself. *Don't make a sound. Or they'll find me!*

A Hunter turned sharply towards her. Her hand went to her back, poised to grab an arrow.

His eyes crinkled, squinting in Safra's direction.

Safra felt an itch in her elbow. Yet, she remained at still as possible. A bead of sweat dripped down her forehead. Had she been discovered?

She ducked down low, behind the thick brush, hoping that she had not seen her.

She looked sideways. Ridan was standing a few feet away. She gave him the signal. *Come on, do something, please,* she said to him silently. *Please understand.*

He nodded. *What if he understood it the wrong way? Oh no.*

His fingers gripped a twig. Taking a deep breath, he threw it at the Hunter's head. "Alcazar! *Zey* are here!"

That was not a Hunter's voice.

It was Neera, the queen.

"Yes, my queen," Alcazar, the Hunter who had been hit by the twig, turned his attention from Safra to Neera. Safra sighed in relief. But now, they were in danger of being discovered.

FORTY-SIX

RACE AGAINST TIME

Safra prayed with all her heart. "Leave. Hunters, please leave," she whispered.

"Search! Keep searching!" Neera said.

"Yes, my queen," Alcazar said.

"Just wait until I get my hands on *zem*!" she exploded. It was impossible to keep quiet. Safra's hand seemed to say to her, "I'll grab the arrow and shoot it in Neera's face! Do it! She imprisoned Raisha and the other men!" But she knew that she would have to stay there. She looked around, watching if anyone had shown the signal. Her hands flinched. Her fingers began to curl impatiently. *I cannot risk it*, she thought.

Her thoughts suddenly directed elsewhere. *Raisha! The men! They must be suffering! Oh no*, she sighed to herself. "Snap out of it, Safra. Watch out if they're sending the signal," she murmured.

But, eventually, the Hunters rode away. *Phew.*

Safra stared at the sky. It was turning a darker shade of blue. She could see the light outline of a moon behind the clouds.

"We've failed!" the Captain walked out of his hiding place. "We can never reach the coast now!"
Chuck and Ahmed were consoling the Captain, saying that it was alright, but they had tears in their own eyes. The Captain had completely broken down. "One more year," he sobbed. "All those years of hard work, and now I have to wait one more year!"

Safra's heart sank. That was it. It was over.
"We've…failed," she murmured. Her knees buckled and she fell to the ground. "That's all I am. I'm a failure." Safra's tears spilled to the ground. She stared at Dayak, who was screeching, "My queen! My queen!"
Ridan was hugging Dayak, and he was crying too. Safra ran over to him. "Ridan…" she started.

"No. I know what you're going to say," he said. But Safra couldn't hold it in. "I'm a failure! Just like what my fear was! It predicted the exact same thing!" She didn't bother to wipe her face. Ahmed and Chuck soon walked to them. The Captain was still devastated. "Poor Captain," Chuck said.
Safra wanted to cry and tell everyone about how she felt, but she had no tears or energy left.

"I am not going to cry again," she muttered to herself. "I'm not going to be a crybaby. I'm going to do something about this!" Safra said out loud. "We have to try."

"Try doing what?" Ridan spat bitterly. "Try what? Huh? Try what?"

"I'll think of something, okay? Don't just stand there!
Why don't you try thinking of something as well?" Safra
snapped back.
"Humph," Ridan scowled.
"So?" Safra tapped her foot, waiting for Ridan's answer.
"How about— we'll just go home?" Ridan said.
"Come on, Ridan!" Ahmed said. "Really, we need a
solution. Be serious."
"Maybe we save Raisha first! She might know what to
do!" Chuck suggested.
"We can't go back there!" Dayak said. "Count me out
of it!"
"It was just a suggestion…"
"Okay. Let's not talk for a while, and just think."
Ahmed sat down and closed his eyes.
They were quiet for a while, until Chuck spoke up again.
"I wish there was a way to, you know, get back to the
Silver Dawn. I mean, time traveling." Ahmed sighed. "I
said, be serious."
The Captain approached them, his head hung low.
"I've got an idea," he said.

FORTY-SEVEN

INSPIRATION

They all sat around in a circle. "Okay Captain, tell us," Ahmed said.

"Well, what Chuck said gave me the idea. Remember the Neera and Meera story? Well, the Guardian mentioned a Rose Scepter that can make any kind of locket. Do you catch my drift?"

"Umm…No," Safra raised an eyebrow.

"Well, my idea is that we make a time-traveling locket!" the Captain said, smiling.

No one said anything. It took a moment for everything to sink in.

"That's brilliant!" Safra said.

"It could work," Ahmed agreed, but still looked a little bit unsure.

Ridan nodded. "But what's the fastest way to get to Neera's castle? It's a moving castle, don't forget. Who knows where it is?" Dayak pointed out.

"That's where I come in," Safra grinned. "We get caught by the Hunters! They'll take us straight to Neera's castle!"

"But, she'll throw us in a dungeon!" Ridan said. "You didn't think of that!"

"Hmmm…Yes." Safra rubbed her chin.

The Captain turned to Dayak. "*You* think of something…*Parrot.*"

"Parrot? How dare you!"

"Oh, sorry. Chicken. No, woodpecker."

"Arrrrgggghh! I am not a woodpecker! I am a peacock. My beak is make of solid gold, my feathers are skeleton keys, and my—"

"Wait, what did you just say?" Safra asked.

"My beak is made of solid gold?"

"Not that."

"My feathers are skeleton keys…?"

"Yes! That's it! We didn't think of this sooner!" Ridan jumped for joy. "We could have easily escaped last time!"

"Yes!" Safra smiled.

"Let's do this," the Captain said.

"Do what?" Dayak looked confused.

"We use your feathers to open the dungeon and escape! It's brilliant!" Chuck laughed.

"I—" Dayak started to say, but Ahmed interrupted him. "Let's find those Hunters. They went…North," he referred to his compass.

"No time to lose. Let's go." the Captain adjusted the cart to make sure that it was well fastened, and he mounted Khan. "Let's get moving!" They loaded their bags, and the rest of them boarded the cart. The Captain said, "Hyah!"

They headed towards the direction that the Hunters had gone. For once, they were looking for the Hunters, instead of hiding from them. "It's ironic, isn't it?" Safra stared at the dark sky, now dotted with stars.

"Ironic what?" Ridan turned to face her.

"It's ironic about how many things that can happen in a day. I've learned so much. And now, everything is completely upside down! We're looking for the Hunters!" Safra laughed. "Can you believe it?"

"I was thinking about Grandpa," Ridan said.

"Uh—" she faltered. "If we get the sand, and we clear everything up, then, we'll go back to Erina sooner than we thought," Safra tried to look at the bright side of the situation.

Ridan didn't answer. He just sighed.

"Ridan…I miss him too," she said.

"I feel guilty for not thinking about him that often." Ridan fiddled with the strap of his bag.

"Oh, Ridan," Safra sighed softly. She wrapped her arm around him. "Look at those stars," Safra said. Ridan looked at her, the little lights reflecting on her eyes. He took a moment to take it all in, his gaze turning towards the full, ripe moon.

"They're so beautiful," she breathed. "One day they're there, and the next night you don't know which is which, expect the big ones," her eyes resting on Polaris. "Mm." Ridan nodded.

"Look at that," she pointed at a band of stars. "There's the constellation Ursa Minor," she said.

"Wow. Grandpa did teach you a lot."

"I know."

They did not exchange a word after that. Both of them drifted off into their own little worlds.

"It's getting darker and darker. Can you see alright?" Ahmed asked. "I can take over for a while." "Yeah, sure," the Captain said.

They exchanged places. The Captain sighed.

"What's wrong, Captain?" Chuck asked.

"I wonder when the Hunters will find us. They're so smart when we don't want to them to be, and now they're not smart when we want them to be."

"Let's stop for a while. It's getting cold," Dayak rubbed his feathers together. "Maybe we can build a fire."

"A fire!" Safra grabbed Dayak and hugged him. "You're a genius!"

"I'm a genius?"

"If we build a fire, then the Hunters will notice the smoke!" Safra said. "Ahmed! Stop!"

Khan halted. "Everyone, gather kindling," the Captain commanded.

"Quick!" All of them hastily grabbed twigs and dried up sticks from the ground. The Captain took out his piece of flint and got to work.

"Chuck! Keep adding those kindling. Try and find some rubber if you can!" the Captain said. "We need a nice, big fire. Not too big, though."

"Yup," Safra said cheerily. Hopefully, their plan would work.

HOOVES

"I hear something," Chuck whispered.

It was the sound of hooves, thudding against the dirt road.

"The Hunters! It worked!" Safra said. "Everyone! Don't hide! Stay on the path!"

They stood there, pretending to not notice the Hunters. Soon enough, they arrived, swords out, spears in hand.

"*Zere* they are!" Neera shouted. "Capture them!"

Safra took one last look at Khan. "Stay hidden, my dear horse," she said. She stuffed some of her important things into her small satchel she hid in the folds of her shirt, remembering to keep a small supply of arrows and her bow, which she slid into the back.

She gave Khan a pat on his head, and gave him a small hug, and she then ran out with the others.

They pretended to panic, while the Hunters tied them up and loaded them onto extra horses. Safra shifted her ropes, so that she could see Neera. The queen took out a black, glossy whistle and blew it. Then, the ground began to rumble. A big shadow rose above them. It was the castle!

She can summon the castle!

"Imprison *zem*!"

They were dragged through corridors, until they finally reached a row of dungeons.

"They all look the same," Safra muttered.

The Hunter roughly threw them into it. "The queen will take care of you later," he growled.

Safra tried to stick her head out of the dungeon to see if Raisha was there, but the bars were too close together.

"Raisha!" she tried whispering, but no avail. "Safra?" the Captain whispered.

"Yeah, what?"

"Is the coast clear?"

"Yes, I believe so."

Ahmed turned to Dayak. "That's your cue," he pushed the bird forwards.

Dayak closed his eyes, and quickly plucked out one of his feathers. He flinched.

"*That* hurts?" the Captain chuckled.

"Try pulling out *your* skin!" Dayak snapped back.

"Uh—" the Captain stuttered.

"Didn't think so," Dayak muttered as he slid his feather in the lock. He hesitated.

"Get on with it," Ahmed said.

"That's…Uh—"

"What?"

"I don't really know if my feathers are skeleton keys!" he blurted out.

"What? You're telling us that now?" the Captain exploded.

"Well, when my queen created me, she only mentioned it," he said, shivering in fear.

"Well try it then!" Safra said, telling herself not to think of the worst situation.

With a trembling beak, he turned it slowly. A small click sound resonated through the hallway.

"Yes!" Safra pumped her fist in the air.

"It worked!" Chuck whispered happily.

They tiptoed out of the dungeon.

"Let's free the other men!" Safra whispered, in hopes of finding Raisha. They walked down a couple of dungeons, where the men were trapped.

"Ben! William! Mark! Leon! Tom!" the Captain gripped the steel bars. "Captain!" they exclaimed. "Dayak! Free them, quickly."

As Dayak turned his head to pluck out another feather, Safra felt a prickling sensation on the back of her neck. *Footsteps!*

"Dayak! Hurry! People are coming!" she hissed.

"Shhhh."

"Dayak! It's too late! Come on!" Ahmed grabbed them and ducked behind a large pillar.

"We can't free them, alas," the Captain said calmly, but Safra could sense pain in his voice.

"I wanted to save Raisha too," Safra said quietly.

"Hmmm," Chuck murmured. Then he spoke up. "Guys," he said.

All of them looked up.

"We have to save Raisha, even if we can't free the men," he said.

"What? Chuck, why are you saying this?" the Captain looked very confused.

"If we want to survive in this quest, then we need Raisha too. There are things we don't know and she knows. We have to find her. Who's with me?" Chuck whisper-shouted.

Safra immediately raised her hand, although she felt bad for the men. *We'll save them later,* she thought. *I'm glad they're okay.* She took a deep breath.

Dayak raised his wing. Ridan glanced at Ahmed. Safra have him a warning look. "I guess I agree," Ahmed said and raised his hand as well. Ridan copied him.

Safra stared at the Captain who didn't move a muscle. She knew that it was hard for him to leave his men behind.

"Captain, please," she said.

He just sighed. Then, he slowly raised his hand.

"Let's go and get 'em!" Chuck said.

FORTY-NINE

THE RESCUE

They poked their heads out from the pillar. Unfortunately, a guard was standing next to the other dungeon.

"Now we still can't save my men!" The Captain muttered.

"Let's focus on saving Raisha," Chuck said.

"This way!" Dayak pointed to a staircase.

"Let's go!" They thudded up the stairs. When they reached the top, their eyes met a wonderful sight. A fountain was set in the middle of the room with a large silver ceiling, held by matching pillars. Soft, black pieces of fabric covered the floor. Safra reached down to touch it.

"They're rose petals!" she exclaimed.

"Black roses! Extraordinary!" Chuck's fingers brushed the soft, silky pieces of the flower.

"Shhhh," the Captain shushed them. He pointed to a lady standing by a giant window, her back to them. Black curls bounced off her shoulders.

"Neera!" Safra whispered in amazement.

"And look!" Chuck exclaimed quietly.

A disheveled, brown-haired girl was tied to a chair.

"Raisha!" Safra longed to run to her and slash her ropes to pieces, but she knew she couldn't.

"Are you going to tell me now?!" Neera thundered.

"No!" Raisha said, trying to appear bold. Safra could sense that she was weak. Her voice said it all.

"You have made the wrong decision," She turned to face Raisha. They ducked behind a sofa, making sure that Neera could not see them. *What is Raisha not telling her? Hmmm,* Safra wondered.

"I won't tell you, no matter what you say!" Raisha shouted, trying to rise from her chair. She fell over, the rope binding her feet tripping her.

"You shall tell me eventually," Neera said. "Alcazar!" The Hunter entered the room. "Yes, my queen?" "Keep checking on *ze* other prisoners. Leave her here, I shall come back. Right now, I have some…Some work, that's all."

"Yes, my queen," Alcazar repeated, and headed in the direction of the dungeons, walking past Safra and the others without noticing them.

"Oh no! They're going to find out that we escaped!" Safra glanced at the disappearing Hunter.

"Then let's go! Neera's leaving!" Ahmed pointed at the queen.

"Wait. She's doing something."

Neera's eyes darted around the room, making sure that no one was there. Then, she turned so Raisha also could not see her, and pressed a tile in the wall. She vanished from sight.

"There's our chance!" Ahmed said and sprung forward, his sword held tightly in his hand. Raisha's eyes widened with surprise.

With a clean slice, her ropes fell to the floor in pieces. She jumped out of the chair, and rubbed her wrists and shoulders. "You guys made it!"

"Yes, of course we did!" Safra said and gave Raisha a hug. "Eww! Stop it!" She shoved Safra to the ground.

"Um. Sorry." Raisha muttered.

"Humph."

"Cut it out! We need to find the Rose Scepter and get out of here!" the Captain said.

"How…How do you know about that?" Raisha's jaw dropped.

"We have no time! They'll find out that we escaped!" Dayak said. "That's a long story. But right now we need to find it, that's all! The Guardian told them everything!"

"Dayak's right!" Safra said.

"I think we should do what Neera did," the Captain walked up to the tile.

"You even know her name? But—"

"Not now, Raisha!" the Captain pressed the tile, and a slab of rock slid open.

"Of course. A secret opening!" the Captain rolled his eyes. "They're almost always there in castles."

"Let's go in. Watch out for Neera, in case she comes back," Safra ignored the Captain's remark.

"Arm yourselves."

They walked in, and all they could see was darkness. "I can't see where I'm putting my foot!" Ridan swatted a bug that had landed in his hair. "Me neither," Safra flailed her hands around wildly, trying to touch the walls to

make sure of where she was going. Then, she
realized could not feel anything under her feet.

"Oh no," Safra muttered as she fell.

FIFTY

THE LABYRINTH

"Uhhhh," Safra groaned. Her whole body ached.

"Ow," Ridan rubbed his ankle.

Safra looked around. A small torch lit the room.

"I guess…We're in heaven? I thought heaven had angels, golden light, clouds, and gods. Wait, what if—" Chuck's eyes widened.

"I don't think it was that big of a fall," the Captain said. "Of course we're not dead."

"Come on, we got to keep going," Raisha started to walk to the next doorway.

"Wait!" Safra said. She carefully lifted the torch from its handle. "This could be useful." She flinched as she held it, a pain searing through her arm. *I must have landed on it,* she thought.

Raisha had noticed that Safra was hurt. She gave her a concerned look, but Safra shook her head. She didn't want to alarm anyone again. "Let's go everybody," she said. The others dusted themselves off and joined Raisha and Safra.

"Go on," the Captain said. Safra took a deep breath and entered the room, holding the torch in front of her. They entered a large, grassy area. The stars shone brightly in the night sky, and a big hedge-like wall made out of vines and leaves towered above them. "Is this— a maze?" Raisha leaned her head to the side. "Yes! It's a… It's a labyrinth!" Safra stared at the path in front of them that led them inside.

Wait, I think I remember something like this. Safra squinted. "I think I must have seen this somewhere," she murmured to herself.

Then it struck her. She had seen this somewhere, but in her own mind. She closed her eyes and concentrated. *My eyes closed. I was sitting in the cabin, back on the ships, and the stone plaque was in my hands. I caressed it, feeling every line.* "I know this! The squiggly lines on the plaque! That's it," she shouted in happiness. She charged right into the maze, torch gripped tightly in her hands.

"Safra! Where are you going!" the Captain walked after her. "Just follow me!" she yelled. She was getting farther and farther away.

"Safra! But—"

"No buts! Follow me, I say," she shouted.

Raisha shrugged and followed her into the labyrinth. The Captain and the others reluctantly did the same. Safra was faced with a choice. *Left or right?*

She closed her eyes again. Every little crack and crevice in the plaque came back to her. She could remember every carved twist and turn, and she was sure of it. They had to turn right.

"Right!" she started to walk faster and faster.

She closed her eyes once more. She remembered that she had felt something, like a little bump on the plaque. Was it an obstacle?

She stopped.

"Did you hear that?" she turned and whispered. "Hear what?"

"That noise. There it is again!" Safra could hear a scratching, itching sound.

"Sounds like— an animal," the Captain whispered.

"Listen closely," Safra said, straining her ear.

"AAAH!" Chuck fell backwards onto the ground.

It was a paw, claws bared. Its silver fur shone as it had just been brushed. It had broken through the labyrinth wall, barely missing Chuck!

"Run!" Safra jumped over the paw. "Go!"

The others, led by Raisha, stumbled after Safra, looking down to their feet to make sure the creature wouldn't appear again.

Safra glanced at the wall next to her. A silver feather stuck out from it.

That's not Dayak's feather, she thought. *Something lurks here. Something here has feathers and sharp claws.*

She picked up her pace. All the way, she kept taking quick looks at the wall.

"Ah!" Ahmed fell over. "The creature! It's on the other side of the wall!" The paw had made another hole in the wall. "Then stay on this side!" Safra yelled, running to him.

"Everyone, crawl through the maze," Raisha ordered. "That way the creature can't claw us."

They obeyed.

The paw kept swiping at them several times, but it could not reach them. The vines were too thick at the bottom for it to break through.

"Keep going," Raisha said, nudging Safra.

Safra felt uneasy, like something was watching her. She turned only to see—

"AAHHH!" she screamed. A pair of orange eyes stared at her through a hole.

"The creature is only on the other side, calm down," the Captain said. "Now, as Raisha said, keep going." "Sorry," she said, and kept crawling.

"But wait," Safra started again. "What if it finds a way to reach this side?"

"Just keep going," Ahmed reassured her.

"Okay. I should calm down," Safra continued along the path, but she still didn't believe Ahmed.

She could hear the vines rustling, but she shook it off, thinking, *I probably just imagined it.*

Then, as she looked at the path ahead of them, she noticed that the wall was coming towards an end. "Wait," she stopped.

"The wall is coming to an end. The creature can come to this side!" Safra said. She spotted the creature coming closer. "Confuse it! Run!" She dashed left and into a rocky path. She looked behind her. No one was there. "They must have run in different paths!" she muttered. "Oh no!"

She kept running, until she came to a dead end.

She took a turn back to the main path. There was no sign of anyone or anything there.

"Guys?" she called out. "Guys?" No answer.

FIFTY-ONE

A CREATURE AND A PALACE

She tried calling them again, but there was no sound, until she heard some leaves rustling.

"Ridan? Captain? Ahmed? Anyone?" Safra felt a pit in her stomach.

"Calm down!" she told herself, gritting her teeth. She closed her eyes and tried to remember the correct path to wherever the destination was.

"Left!" she took a quick turn, where she was blinded by bright silver light.

She squinted, and the light partially faded. She opened her eyes, only to come face-to-face with the creature itself. Its burning amber eyes stared into her.

"It's a silver lion!" Safra stared at its glistening mane. Her gaze shifted to the giant feathery wings that extended from its back, and then she spotted its claws. She knew that she was standing in front of a dangerous lion that could kill her any minute. Her fingers worked quickly to ready her bow, but before she could even grab an arrow, the lion swiped at her. Safra escaped from its clutches in the last second, its claws making a small rip in her shirt. As she backed up, she could see the rest of them behind the creature, far away. She could see the shocked looks on their faces.

"I must get to them!" she grunted and shot an arrow at the lion's wing. It dodged it by folding it away. It then growled and swiped at her again. She jumped out of the way, but its other claw had been waiting for her.

Safra felt a searing pain explode in her leg. "Ah!" she fell to the ground, helpless.

The lion, realizing that she was hurt, bent in for the kill, teeth bared. It was so close to her that she could smell its stinky breath. "Well, I guess I know that you didn't brush your teeth this morning," she chuckled nervously.

"*Zordon!*" A velvety voice called out. Safra's eyes widened. "It can't be…"

The lion turned. "Is *zat* some mouse or something? Leave it and come!" the voice called again. "Neera?" Safra murmured. "She's coming back!" Safra scrambled behind a wall, so that she couldn't be seen. She peered out, and saw Neera passing, with Zordon at her heels. "Come, my pet. Mommy will feed you," she cooed as she disappeared.

The others emerged from hiding and ran over to Safra. "Phew, that was close," the Captain said. Raisha sat down next to Safra. "You're hurt," she said, and put her hands on Safra's wound. Green light flashed for a moment. "All better," she said.

"Raisha, how did you—" Ahmed's jaw dropped. "She's a Healer," Safra interrupted. She stood up and shook her leg back and forth. She smiled at Raisha warmly. "You are getting better at this thing. It healed faster!"

"Oh, no," Raisha said, "I'm not very good."

"Quit gaping, everyone. We have to go," the Captain said. "Safra, lead the way!"

"I'm on it, Captain," she said, and closed her eyes once more. They took twists and turns, until Safra could feel that they were close.

"One more turn to the right!" she said, and walked ahead.

"Guys! COME! Quickly!" Safra shouted.

"Is it another creature?" the Captain rushed to Safra's side, his hand gripping his sword.

"Wow! This is, this is magnificent!" his grip on the sword faltered and it clattered to the ground.

They were standing on a sleek, marble floor. A few feet away, a small but beautiful palace stood in front of them. Beautiful glass windows were placed everywhere. A small pool of glistening, clear water surrounded it.

The others had reached by that time. "Wow. Just wow." Ridan stared at the beautiful masterpiece.

"Let's go inside," Safra said and walked forward. Raisha caught up to her.

"Thanks," she said.

"Thanks for what?" Safra turned to look at her. "Chuck told me that you were the one who told them to help save me instead of your men," Raisha said somewhat reluctantly.

"You're welcome," Safra said and smiled. "Now let's finish this adventure."

FIFTY-TWO

INSIDE THE PALACE

Safra entered the doorway. "I think this is where the first half of the Rose Scepter is," Safra said. She could recognize the musty smell. "This is the place where I had a vision."

She spotted a black stone corridor. Without a word, she began walking towards it, her hand coming in contact with the walls. She glanced at the beautiful silver ornaments that hung overhead. Safra focused on what was in front of them. *A stained glass door, huh?*

Safra stepped up to and raised her foot, but hesitated. She knew she had to do it, but it was a pity to destroy such a work of art.

She smashed the glass. Shards of the color fell to the floor. "Safra—" the Captain called, but stopped. He stared in awe as she stepped into the room behind the glass.

Safra stared at the silken black cloth covering the room. It was exactly like the vision! She could see the object on the table.

"Wait." Safra tried to recall what had happened next.
"Oh no! Footsteps!" She could hear them, exactly the way
they were in her vision.

"No!" Safra ducked underneath a fold of cloth. She
beckoned the others to hide as well. Then, the footsteps
faded away.

"Phew," Safra got up from her hiding place. "That was
really close," she murmured.

The rest of them got up as well. "I think that's the Rose
Scepter!" Ahmed ran to the table. "Wait! You need to
turn the table—" Raisha started.

Ahmed uncovered the object. Silver light glowed faintly
from it.

"It's a staff!" Ahmed gripped it in his hand. "Wow!"
Raisha inspected it. "That was peculiar! But, yes. This is it.
The first half of the Rose Scepter!" She took it from
Ahmed, gently caressing the silver object. "Let's go. We
can't risk the guards coming after us."

"*Zere* won't be a need for guards." Everyone stiffened.

"Aunt Neera." Raisha's hand held the staff even tighter.

"Aunt?" Safra turned to face her.

"Yes! Didn't you figure it out yet? Meera is my mother!"
Raisha said bitterly, a tear glistening in her eye. She
brushed it away.

"Raisha." Neera's eyes narrowed at the sight of the rest
of them. "Hello again, my friends."

"Hello," Safra said through clenched teeth. *We are not your
friends, and we never will be!*

"I thought you left in the labyrinth," Ridan spoke up.

"Oh! Of course, I knew *zat* you were there. I also was the
one who saved you from Zordon," she pointed a finger at

Safra. "But why would you do that?" Safra said, trying to keep calm, although her blood was boiling with anger. "Oh? Simply," Neera chuckled. Safra curled her fingers into fists at her sides. "But you let us get your part of the Rose Scepter!" Raisha said. "*Zen* what do you think this is?" Neera banged the staff she held in her hand on the floor. "It's a fake!" She pointed to the one Raisha held. "I'm always one step ahead of my enemies," Neera glared at Raisha. "Especially when *zey* don't cooperate." Raisha dropped the fake one onto the floor. "You tricked us!"

"*Zat's* life, sweetie. Learn to live it." Neera blew a kiss, and snapped her fingers. She disappeared.

"Wait!" Raisha cried.

"What does Neera want from you?" Safra asked. "Only I know where my mother's half of the Scepter is. It's hidden in her castle. Neera wants the other half of the Rose Scepter again, that's why. One, because she wants to make more lockets. Two, because she doesn't want us to break the curse." Raisha sighed. "But we need Mother's locket."

"I have it," Safra took it out from her pocket. "I found it in the North Tower."

"All we need is time," the Captain said. "It's dawn." Safra looked out of the window. Stars still dotted the dark sky. "You mean, this is the Silver Dawn?" Silver shooting stars fell gracefully.

"Yes! Look at those!" the Captain gasped at the sight of the shooting stars. Silver streaks flashed through the night.

"Beautiful." Safra smiled.

"And now our only hope is the Rose Scepter," Raisha said. "Every Silver Dawn, the sun will never rise, and the night will rule."

Safra could now see why it was called the Silver Dawn. "Raisha, take us to your mother's castle."

FIFTY-THREE

SAFRA'S LESSON

They dashed out of the maze and back into Neera's room. "Let's get out of here!" Safra cried. "There's a window!" Ridan pointed. They climbed out with the help of a tree.

"Okay, Raisha, it's your time to shine! How do we get to your mom's castle?"

"It is hidden deep in the River Valley," she said, "which lies beyond," she pointed to a group of bright green and gray mountains. "It is there. My home is there." She sighed wistfully. "We must walk."

They all groaned. "Walking, here we come," Chuck said sarcastically.

"I wish Khan was here," Safra said. "Too bad we left him behind. When Raisha gave her a confused look, she explained. "He's one of the Hunter's horses."

"Oh." Raisha looked at her feet, silent.

"Well, um… I was hoping… if you would tell me more about…you know," Safra began.

"I know, I know. You are wondering how I became trapped in that lake down below in the forest." Raisha sighed. "All right, I shall tell you. When my mother was cursed, I was a mere child. I was raised by my mother's closest friend, a woman by the name of Zelda. My mother trusted her so much that she even gave her a Seer locket as well. Oh, once I even believed she was my own mother! But, she kept a secret from me. One day, I heard Zelda talking to someone about my mother's curse, which no one had told me about. I ran away, vowing that I would find my mother's locket and I would free her. I was almost sure that my aunt had it." She took a deep breath.

"But in the forest, when I was trying to conquer my fear, Hunters came and sabotaged it. Neera tried to force me to tell her where the other half of the Scepter was, but I refused. They started to scare and taunt me, and I was sucked into the cave. They filled it up with water, thinking that I would drown. I stayed there for a long time, until…Until you found me." She smiled. "And now I have true hope of freeing my mother."

Safra smiled back. "We will free her, that's for sure." She turned to look at the great peaks that lay in front of them. They reached a great cliff that overlooked the valley. "It's like the cliff back at home," Safra breathed, the feeling of homesickness washing over her. She felt a hand on her shoulder. It was Ridan. He nodded, acknowledging her pain. Safra tilted her head to the side. "The castle!"

An amazing structure made of white marble stood in front of them. Large turrets sparkled, contrasting against the inky night. Gemstones adorned the sides of the main entrance.

"Wow," Safra dropped the backpack that she was
holding.

"But wait. There's a problem I think you guys should
see," Ridan said, and pointed into the distance. Safra
gasped.

"It's the Hunters! They've beaten us to it!" Raisha
sighed. A big group of Hunters surrounded the castle,
with swords and spears.

"We can't fail!" Safra cried out. "We can't!"

The Captain sighed. "Not this failure thing again." "Safra,
you need to know something." Ahmed said. "I appreciate
that you don't want to give up and everything, but you
need to know that you shouldn't always think about
failing."

"Ahmed's correct," Chuck stepped in. "We need to
think about the solutions first before thinking about
failing. I know, I know, you do have a lot of solutions.
But, every single time we encounter a hard obstacle, you
think and talk about failing first."

"Safra, remember, you must be confident. Stop thinking
about failing, and think about solving." the Captain
smiled. "Now, let's think of a solution."

Safra nodded. She took a deep breath. *Don't think of failing,*
she told herself.

"We can sneak into the castle!" she said. "Only Raisha
knows where it is, right? We take it, and somehow get
Neera's staff too!" Safra said.

"But we need a solid plan," Ridan said.

"No, we don't. Let's wing it," Safra said. "Just go with
the flow! We'll think of something along the way, because
we don't have time."

"That's a good idea," Ridan said.

"Yes," Chuck said.

"We are definitely going to beat those Hunters!" Raisha said.
"I agree." the Captain said, and they set off for the castle.

FIFTY-FOUR

WINGING IT

"Okay, now how do we sneak past these Hunters?" Safra scratched her chin.

"Easy. The classic distraction." the Captain grabbed Dayak. "Ok, you can fly, right? Go and rustle those bushes. Go!"

"O— ok," Dayak stammered and hid himself behind a bush.

"Wait for it," the Captain whispered.

Dayak did as he was told. He rattled it with his beak.

"Hey! There's something there!" Several Hunters went over to examine the bush.

"Now!" the Captain grabbed them and they ran towards the door. "Intruders!" Other Hunters went after them.

"Hunters are behind us! Faster!" Raisha led them into a corridor. "There's a closet here!" All of them tried to squeeze into a tiny room.

"Whoo! I'm surprised that I remembered this place," Raisha wiped her forehead.

"Yuck! Ahmed! Your foot is near my mouth!"

"Sorry Chuck. I can't see you."

"Oh, right."

"Umm…Ahem. We left Dayak behind," Safra said. "Oh, I already had a plan for that," the Captain said sheepishly. "Uh… We wait for the Hunters to pass, and then we go and get him."

"Ugh! Captain! We don't know where he is!" Safra frowned.

"He's probably just flying somewhere," the Captain chuckled nervously.

Safra gave him a warning look. "Okay, my bad," he said. "But we'll save him for sure."

"I think the coast is clear," Raisha said. "Let's get out of here."

They quietly tiptoed out of the closet. "Okay. Now for Dayak," Safra said.

"I'm glad you remembered me." A rather cross looking albino peacock stood there, leaning on a pillar. "Dayak! Phew. Let's go, quick!" Safra grabbed him. "Raisha, show us the way to the Rose Scepter!"

"It's this way. We must go up to Mother's chamber," Raisha said. "It's upstairs… But it's also downstairs…Whatever. Just forget what I said." "Okay, then let's go," the Captain said. "But…" Raisha hesitated. "But what?"

"There's a small complication," Raisha pointed up, towards many staircases that went so high they seemed to disappear. "I don't know which one."

"What? But you said you knew!" "Oh no!" Dayak panicked.

"I know I said that, but… These staircases were always hard to navigate. I'll have to eyeball it." Raisha tried to force herself to smile, but it came out more like a grimace.

FIFTY-FIVE

THE TUNNEL

"This is going on forever!" Ridan said, panting. They had been climbing the same staircase for over an hour, and they still could not see the top.

Safra sat down on one of them. "Whoo," she gasped for breath. "I need a moment to rest."

"I'm tired as well," Chuck collapsed next to Safra. "I wish it were as easy as going down. We could just slide down the banister." Ahmed sighed as he did the same. "Ahmed! It *is* that easy!" Safra jumped up from her spot. "We can use the spindles as a ladder. We can climb way easier! And once we're close enough, we can see where the staircases are leading us. Then, we can switch to the one that's the right one!" Safra jumped in joy. "It's brilliant, I must say," the Captain said. "Let's try it." He slid his leg carefully over the rail, and gripped the spindle, planting his legs firmly so he would not fall. Then, he began to climb it. "Wow! This is amazing!" the Captain shouted. In seconds, he was gone.

"Let's go then! Did you see how fast the Captain did that?" Ridan did the same. He quickly followed the Captain's path.

Safra shrugged and followed him. They switched to a few other staircases before they found the right one. "That's the one! That door, over there!" Raisha cried. "Only a few more rungs," Ahmed said.

They soon reached the top. "Well, that was easy!" Safra panted. "Let's get that Rose Scepter!"

"Okay. Now, this is why Neera wants me. It's not a fancy secret passageway or anything, but it's this." Raisha kicked off the rug that lay on the floor. She stamped her foot on one of the tiles, and it lowered, uncovering a dark tunnel.

"There's an underground tunnel that leads all around Silver Island. I know it like the back of my hand." Raisha smiled. "Climb in!" Safra gingerly stepped down. The rest of them followed her inside. "Mother's chamber is here." Safra could not see Raisha's face, but she could tell that she was upset.

"It's okay," Safra said. "I've lost a mother and father. But I have a grandpa, and I'm happy that my life's the way it is."

"You have?" She felt Raisha's hand on her shoulder. "Oh, I'm really sorry."

"It's fine."

Nobody said anything.

"So, are you happy about being a Healer?" Ahmed asked, trying to start a conversation. "I actually wished to be a Seer, like my mother," Raisha said rather sharply. "Uh—" Safra knew that Ahmed regretted asking that question.

"It's okay. I'll develop my powers sooner or later. I can only heal small cuts and bruises." She sighed.

"Well, I would love to be a Healer," Ridan said. "I think it's pretty cool."

Raisha sighed again. Safra felt sorry for her.

"Let's keep going," she just said.

They kept walking. "Awkward," Dayak squawked quietly in Safra's ear.

"Shhhh. Keep quiet, you silly bird!" Safra hissed to him. It seemed that Raisha had heard him. She turned to look at them, a cross look on her face.

Safra gritted her teeth. Things weren't going so well. She decided to formulate a plan for getting the staff from Neera.

"Hey, Ahmed," she called.

"What?"

"Do you still have the fake Scepter?" she asked. "I think Chuck has it."

"Hmmm…" Safra murmured. "Chuck? Do have the fake Scepter?"

"Yes." It floated towards her.

"This will be more useful than we think it will." Safra chuckled quietly to herself. But her thoughts were interrupted by Raisha.

"Here we are. This is the place."

FIFTY-SIX

THE OTHER HALF

Safra stared at the white and silver door that lay in their way, and watched Raisha slowly twist the doorknob. She could hear Raisha whisper to herself— "Mother— are you here?"

They walked in. A beautiful canopy bed with silver shades was in the middle, and a wardrobe at the side. Safra turned to see a glass table, where an object covered in white silk cloth was placed.

"It's the head of the Rose Scepter!" Safra gasped. "Take it! Quick!" Chuck said. "I don't like this tunnel place very much."

"Wait. Turn, and then remove the cloth," Raisha murmured. She turned the table which spun elegantly, and when it came to a stop, Raisha unveiled it. "Wow!" the Captain gasped. A magnificent rose made out of silver rested on the glass.

"Oh my goodness!" Raisha gasped. "It's more stunning than I thought! See? We always turn the table before we take off the cloth. I had a small doubt when Ahmed took the fake one out, because he didn't spin it," she said. They all nodded.

Raisha picked it up slowly, running her fingers against the smooth metal. "Quickly! Hide it!" Safra said. Raisha grabbed a robe from her mother's closet and donned it. She concealed the rose beneath it and hooked it to her belt as well.

"Okay. Now we need to get the other half from Neera," the Captain said.

"I already have a plan for that," Safra smiled. "If Neera ever puts down the staff, we can switch it with the fake one that we have. That way, we have enough time to escape safely before she finds out the truth."

"That is a good idea, but what if Neera doesn't put down the staff?" Ridan scratched his head.

"Then we'll just have to distract her," Safra said.

They walked out of the chamber. She turned and noticed that Raisha was lingering in the back.

"Raisha—" she started, but stopped. She could see her looking around the room.

She must miss her mother. I'm lucky. I don't remember mine. But still, I wish that Mom and Dad were here, Safra thought.

"Raisha!" Safra called reluctantly. They had to keep going.

"Oh. I got a little carried away." She followed Safra back into the tunnel.

"Okay. Now we have to spy on Neera," Ridan said. They slowly climbed out of the tunnel and back into the room. They slowly tiptoed towards the staircases, which the Hunters and Neera were ascending. "Hide!" They dashed into a room, and poked their heads out.

Neera collapsed on the stairs. "Oh, I can't go farther," she moaned.

Safra and Ridan snickered. "Hehe," Safra tried to stifle her laughter. "Poor lady."

Ridan clapped his hand over his mouth.

"Wait." Safra said. "Look."

Neera got up. "I must have water," she said. She slowly started to descend.

"Oh no. We're stuck here!" Ahmed said, alarmed. "We need to go downstairs," Raisha said. "I think we should fight them."

"Hmmm. Maybe two or three of us could sneak downstairs and the rest should fight," Ridan said. "Safra, Ridan, Raisha. The three of you are responsible for getting the staff from Neera. The rest of us shall fight," the Captain said. "Come on, everyone. Escape when the Hunters look distracted."

Safra gave him the thumbs up sign, and the rest of them sprang out of their hiding place, armed with their weapons.

The Hunters also armed themselves, and began to fight. "Guys! Slide down the banisters!" Safra yelled as she swung her leg over the rail and slid past the fighting that was going on. Raisha and Ridan followed her.

"There she is!" Safra pointed to Neera, who was drinking water from a goblet.

"I have to do this," Raisha said. She handed the fake staff to Safra. "Take it."

Raisha snuck around the room, and stood in front of Neera. "I will tell you where the other half is." She raised her hands up in surrender.

Neera dropped her goblet in surprise. She adjusted her cloak and tried to regain her composure. "Why so sudden? Is *zis* some kind of trick?" She sneered. "No chance, sweetie, I'm not falling for that!"

"Then fight with me first!" Raisha brandished a sword. Neera did not hesitate for a moment. She dropped the staff to the ground and took out a sword of her own. "Do you *zink* you can beat *me*?"

"Yes!" Raisha sprung forward.

Safra quickly ran out in the open and took the staff. She tossed it to Ridan, and replaced it with the fake one. She caught Raisha's gaze for a second, and Safra nodded. Raisha quickly blocked Neera's swipe at her, and ran back to the stairs. She motioned them to follow her.

When they reached the top, all the Hunters were lying down on the ground, and the Captain, Ahmed, and Chuck were panting. "They might get up at any moment! Let's find a safe place!" Raisha said. "Safra and Ridan got the staff! The armory is this way. We'll lock it."

FIFTY-SEVEN

THE ARMORY

They walked into a room, filled with armor and weapons. "Whoa," Safra breathed.

"Yes, it's beautiful, is it not?" Raisha's fingers brushed against the smooth metal of a shield with a crest of a peacock engraved on it.

"It's splendid!" The Captain seemed to be dazzled by all the weapons. "They're…They're so fine! Such quality!" he marveled. He hesitated, and then asked, "May I?"

"Yes!" Raisha said. The Captain unsheathed a couple of swords. "Whoa," he twirled the shiny objects.

"The door's locked. Okay, so now what do we do? Make the locket?" Ridan asked.

"Yes, but it's not simple, I warn you," Raisha said. She took a deep breath. "Okay. Let's take out the two parts," she said, "and we have to connect both of them."

"And then you just think of any locket we want and it'll make it?" Safra asked.

"Oh, no no! There's a little hole on the bottom of the
Head of the Scepter. We have to put something in it."
Raisha said. "What's that something?" Ridan asked.
 "Be patient. Hmmm…Well, it's hard to explain. You see,
if you wanted to make a Healer locket, you would put
a *tulsi* leaf, or *holy basil*, inside the hole. Then you spin the
staff in place, and it it's made!" Raisha said. "For a
Whisperer locket, you would need the tooth of any
animal. And then, for the Seer locket, you would have to
use a small piece of elephant skin, because they have such
good memories. Now, the elephant skin is really hard to
find."
 "That's why Neera couldn't make it!" Safra exclaimed.
"Yes, yes. She tried to substitute it with other substances.
That's another story." Raisha explained. "Now, if we
want to time travel, how would we do it?"
 "Wait. Let's make a test first." They made a locket using
a small, dried up leaf. It worked!
 "Don't bother using it anymore. All it does is glow
plants rapidly. Safra, just keep it with you," Raisha said.
"We need something that represents time," the Captain.
"All of us were too silly not to bring a pocket-watch!"
Safra's heart sank. She pulled out her shiny silver pocket-
watch and sighed.
"I have one," she said. She closed her eyes so nobody
could see the tears forming.
"But…But that's Grandpa's!" Ridan said.
Safra had no answer.
 "Safra— you don't have to do it. We'll find some other
thing—"
 "No Raisha. Take it. It's the only way. Besides, maybe
Grandpa will buy me another one," she said, although
she knew that this pocket-watch was irreplaceable.

"Safra..." the Captain started.

"I insist," she interrupted and placed it in Raisha's palm. "Let's do this." She quickly brushed away the water from her eyes so nobody would notice.

"If you're okay with it," Raisha shrugged and placed the pocket-watch inside the hole. She slowly fit the staff inside the head, and began to turn it.

"I hope it works," the Captain said.

No one said anything back. Silence filled the room.

"Why isn't anything happening?" Ahmed stared at the Scepter. It stayed as still as ever.

"Wait for a few—"

Before Raisha could finish her sentence, a blast of silver light came from the top of the head of the Scepter! It danced against the walls, making them look like a kaleidoscope. Then the head turned once, and went still.

"It worked!" The Captain said as Raisha slowly unscrewed the top.

She put her hand inside the head, and slowly took out a glistening locket. Everyone was speechless.

FIFTY-EIGHT

THROUGH TIME

"Yes! Now we can break the curse and get the silver sand too!" Chuck cheered. Safra couldn't help but smile. "Yes, but this is not the time to celebrate. We must find a way to get out of here." The Captain tried to be serious. "Let's start thinking. Wait— what was that?" The door rumbled with a powerful impact.

"The Hunters!" Raisha gasped.

"Quick! I have an idea!" Safra said. "Let's just go back in time now, with the locket. We'll figure out how it works later. We'll use it and hope for the best!"

"Safra— we don't know if it works properly. What it isn't the way we think it will work?" Ahmed said. "Now there's a point," the Captain said. "But we have to try," Raisha said. "There are no windows here. If the Hunters get in here — we're toast. We can't fight like this, protecting the Scepter and ourselves as well!"

The Captain seemed to be in deep thought. But, after a while, he nodded. "Who is to wear the locket?" he asked.

"You should, Captain," Safra said. "Ridan, Raisha, and I have lockets already."

He took it from Raisha. "No. I'm giving the Ahmed the honor." When everyone looked at him suspiciously, he said, "No! It's not the way you think it is! I'm not scared, I just thought—"

"It's okay, Captain. We're just kidding." Safra clapped him on the back. She took the locket and put in Ahmed's hand. "Put it on."

He seemed to hesitate for a second before putting it on. "Remember, the locket activates when it thinks you're worthy of it." Raisha said. "We have to wait for a while."

"Okay," Ahmed said quietly. Safra sensed that he was nervous. His hands trembled slowly at his sides. He noticed that she was staring at him, and immediately stuffed them into his pockets.

Safra opened her mouth to say something, but paused. She took a deep breath instead and decided to wait. The Captain sighed. "How much longer?" Then, as on cue, a white light burst from the locket. It had activated! It formed into the shape of the pocket-watch.

"It's happening!" Safra said.

Raisha smiled. "Yes!"

"I wonder how it activated so soon…Well, I guess it's time. Let's use it!"

"Careful," the Captain said immediately. "Umm…how are all of us going to time travel if only Ahmed's wearing the locket?" Ridan asked.

"Good question," Raisha said. "Hmmm…I can't believe we didn't think of that!"

"Maybe he has to be in contact with us. When we're time traveling, Ahmed has to hold on to us so we'll go with him!" Chuck said.

"We don't know if that's going to work." The Captain crossed his arms.

Safra rolled her eyes. She held on to Ahmed's bag. "You don't have to if you don't want to," she said to the Captain. "You can stay behind."

The rest of them chuckled and held on to Ahmed as well. "I…I change my mind," the Captain said and copied the others.

Ahmed closed his eyes. "Come on…come on…" he muttered quietly.

"Come on, Ahmed," Chuck said.

"I've never worn a *necklace* before!" Ahmed snapped through clenched teeth.

"Okay, calm down. Let the feeling come naturally," Raisha said. "Just don't think about anything else."

Ahmed sat down. "Okay, okay." He took a deep breath. "Wait. How far back in time should we go? Maybe when Ridan and I were in the Cove?" Safra asked.

"No! At that time Raisha would still be inside the cave! She would not be with us," Chuck said. "Makes sense," Safra agreed.

Safra felt like she was vibrating. She stared at her hands and feet, which were trembling uncontrollably. "Some—something's going on!" Her teeth started to chatter. A powerful gust of wind began to blow around them.

"I—I think it's working!" Chuck shouted over the sound.

"I can't hear anything!" Safra shouted.

"What—What?" Ridan yelled.

"Huh?"

"What did you say?"

"What? The wind is too strong!"

"Whatever! Both of you be quiet!" the Captain shouted.

"WHAT?" Ridan and Safra shouted at the same time.

"Never mind," the Captain muttered.

"Go back a few hours before the dawn happened!" Ahmed shouted at the top of his lungs.

Then, the wind stopped.

FIFTY-NINE

THE PROBLEM

Safra looked around. It was night, and they were standing next to a fire. "It worked!"

"We're in the place where the Hunters caught us. Even Khan is still here!" The Captain pointed to a sleeping horse.

"First, we have to get to the Cove! But…Why are we here? I thought the locket would take us to the coast!" Ahmed scratched his head.

"Well, you never said that!" Safra corrected.

"Then let's try it again," Ridan said.

And so they tried it once more, but this time Ahmed told the locket to take them to the coast. The wind stopped.

"We're still in the same place!" Safra sighed.

"Why isn't it working?

"Because pocket-watches don't represent that," Ahmed said. "I guess we have to just try to get to the coast in time."

"We have Khan, but it still won't be enough to get to the coast," Raisha said. "I'm afraid that we have to think of something else. Plus, the Cove is still far away from the coast."

"But…But it can't be," Safra slammed her bag to the ground. "How are we going to do this now?" Her fur coat had fallen out of the bag, and Safra remembered something. A dizzy feeling overcame her, and she fell to the ground.

I close my eyes, and I've opened them in another world. It was a vision. I knew it.

I'm standing in a cold place. Zelda's place!

The house and Zelda had faded away. I stare at the bag of Azella seeds in my hand.

Everything fades.

"Ah!" Safra shook her head and sat up. "It was a vision," she explained to the others, who were looking at her, bewildered.

"Well, what did you see?" Ahmed asked.

"I just saw something from the past," she answered, "Something when Zelda disappeared. I was holding the Azella seeds."

"Zelda? You know where she is? And Azella seeds? Those…Those are so rare!" Raisha jumped up and down.

Safra extracted the pouch from her bag. "Here they are," she handed it to Raisha.

"Don't any of you get it? We can use the Azella to get to the Cove! All we have to find is a snowy place! And, this is important."

"Yes! Yes! The Captain said. "We must go back to the Rede Mountains!"

"It is going to be quite the struggle," Ahmed said. But you're right. All we have to do is get near some snow. "That's all."

"Now quick! We must get going before the Hunters find us! Remember? They'll find us! Safra, distinguish the fire. I'll get Khan ready." The Captain harnessed the cart to the horse and loaded the rest of their bags in it. Safra hurried over to them and jumped in the cart.

She beckoned Raisha to come and sit next to her. She gave Safra a warm smile and squeezed between the bags. "We're in for a ride!" Safra smiled back.

"Yes. I actually can't believe that this is actually happening! You all are such gracious people, helping me without any reason!" Then her smile faded. Wait…There is a reason. The sand. Of course."
She turned away from Safra.

"Even if we couldn't get the sand, I would definitely help you," Safra said quickly. She placed a hand on Raisha's shoulder. "Please don't judge. I didn't come here expecting to be involved in a complicated story circled around a dangerous curse, I came here have adventure, and make my grandfather proud. I wanted to fulfill my dreams."

Raisha did not reply. She seemed to be suddenly very interested in her hair.

Safra just sighed and turned to stare at the landscape as they took off.

"Fine! If that's the way you think of us!" Safra muttered angrily.

SIXTY

BREAKING IT

As they approached the Rede Mountains, the silence became more intense. Safra didn't feel like forgiving Raisha, and the rest of them didn't want to mess with her.

 "Safra! Give me a break! I had my reasons to say that!"
"And I have my reasons not to forgive you. You think that we're just a bunch of self-centered jerks!" she said coldly.

 "Just come on!" Raisha slumped back in her seat.

 "It was your fault anyway!" Dayak said.

 "You too?" She turned to him.

 "Everyone, just stop talking about this," the Captain snapped. "Now it's annoying."

"Look on the bright side. We'll reach the mountains faster because of Khan," Ahmed said, but nobody replied.

 Soon, they could see the mountains appearing. "There it is!"

The Captain urged Khan to go faster. Safra dug her fingers through the seeds in the pouch. "I hope it'll work," she murmured.

"Of course it's going to work," Ridan said.

"There! There's the first sign of snow!" Ahmed said.

"Go for it, Safra," he said.

She stepped out of the cart with the seeds in hand. Safra kneeled down and buried the seed in the snow.

"Come on guys! This is the time!" A small orange flower sprouted instantly.

They all gathered round. All of them held hands as Safra picked the flower and yelled, "Take us to the Silver Serpent Cove!"

A gust of wind circled them.

As it faded away, they opened their eyes, and they stood there, their shoes sinking in the sand. The scorching sun beat down on them. The sudden change in the weather gave Safra a dizzy, surprised feeling.

"Feels good to be back in normal climate," the Captain said.

"There's the cave!" Safra exclaimed. "But be quiet. There are some hyena-like creatures here that are out to get us. Be really quiet."

"There's one!" Ahmed pointed to a flash of black that had disappeared behind some trees.

"Go!" Safra dashed into the clearing and jumped into the cave. She motioned for the others to follow her.

And so they went, one by one, into the cave. The Captain gasped as he entered. "Wow…This…This is amazing!" His gaze landed on the drawing of Meera. "She looks just like…Neera."

Raisha walked up to the portrait and stared at it. She slowly touched it, and it glowed.

She quickly took it away, like she had been burnt.
"She…She feels real!" she gasped. Meera gave Raisha the same wistful smile.
"Mom?" She touched the drawing again. "First, we must break the curse," Ahmed said. "Do it, Safra."
Safra looked at the sky. Dawn was starting. She took out the locket, edged closer to the drawing, and unclasped it. She stood on her tiptoes and slowly pressed the locket to Meera's neck.
A powerful blast of air pushed Safra back. She landed with a hard thud on the floor. "Ow," she dusted herself off. A powerful blue and white light filled the room. All of them hurried to cover their eyes. A mixture of sand and dust started to form, swirling around the room.
All of them began to cough violently, falling to the ground. Safra tried desperately to open her eyes, and then the dust settled down, and the light faded.
All of them gasped and stood up. An elegant woman stood in front of them. Her brown hair bounced on her shoulders, and her billowing white robes seemed to glow. A smile formed on her lips. Her hazel eyes blinked slowly, like a flickering candle.
Safra stared at the sky. Silver flashes zoomed against the inky indigo, amongst the stars. The dawn seemed to be brighter than ever, but they knew that it would soon become morning again. The last Silver Dawn would be over, now that the curse was broken.
Raisha immediately hugged Meera, who hugged her back.
Dayak bowed in respect. "My queen."
"Dayak, I sense that you have done well." She stroked his feathers affectionately.

Meera turned to face the rest of them. They all took a step back. "Use extreme caution," the Captain whispered. "Don't worry. I know you are doubtful of me, but, I must thank you all first. I remember these two, though." Meera pointed to Ridan and Safra.

Safra felt like she could fall asleep by hearing her voice. It was so soothing.

"I— I'm so sorry," the Captain removed his hat. "I did not mean to offend you."

"Oh, don't apologize. I thank you all again. Now, I must ask about your adventure."

And so, they explained everything, from start to finish. Meera watched them with great interest, staying silent all the while.

"So you used a pocket-watch! Brilliant!" she said.

"Yeah," Safra sighed.

Meera snapped her fingers, and the locket faded away, leaving only the pocket-watch!

"Oh!" Safra was speechless.

"Wait. Why is there a floating coat there?" she asked, motioning to Chuck.

"That's Chuck. He drank a large amount of water from the Sun Oasis," Raisha explained. Meera closed her eyes and swirled her hand around, and Chuck slowly reappeared.

"Yes!" Ahmed patted Chuck on the back. "He's back!" They cheered, hugging and playfully hitting Chuck.

"So Neera is involved in this?" Meera started again. "I'm afraid so, my queen," Dayak said. "What they have said is true."

"Well, you all have earned this," Meera said. She handed them the bracelet with the key on it. "You may collect the silver sand!" She smiled brightly, but Safra could sense a

tint of urgency and concern in her voice, and she could
see that the others could too.

They began to celebrate. But, then, it all sank in.

"We want to finish this off." Safra said.

"I don't feel complete," Chuck said. "This adventure
doesn't feel complete."

"I...I do not understand," Meera stammered.
"Mother, they want to go with you and help defend
against Aunt Neera." Raisha explained.

"All right." Meera sighed. "Let us go."

"Yes!" Safra said and pumped her fist.

SIXTY-ONE

THE ATTACK

"But, you must know that I do not approve very much of this." Meera said. "Neera will come. I know."
"She doesn't know that we're here. In all due respect, I think that we are safe for now." Dayak said.
"The hyena creatures serve Neera. They should have seen us by now." Meera took a look out of the cave. "But then they would have attacked." Safra scratched her head. "They did last time."
"At that time they did not recognize you. They may have seen Raisha, and would have reported it to her. Neera would be on her way."
Safra sighed. *Whoa, this is complicated.*
"Let's go. We'll stand on the shore, and we'll await her arrival." Meera walked out of the cave, her robes swishing against the ground. She seemed somewhat occupied. Chuck shot Safra a look, but she just shrugged and followed her out of the cave.

The stiff, salty breeze ran through her hair. She stared at
the beautiful sea, which she had missed so much. She
took a deep breath, taking it all in.

"And there she comes," Meera pointed to a black
rowboat heading towards them. Four Hunters were
rowing, with Neera standing next to them, fuming. The
hand that usually held her staff was curled into a little ball,
red from the pressure. Her bold but beautiful face was
twisted in a hard frown.

"All of you go hide behind those bushes. Do not come
out!!" Meera said.

The boat reached the shore.

"I see *zat* you are back, sister," Neera sneered. She
motioned the Hunters to go away. They rowed to other
side and began to dock.

"Do not call me your sister!" Meera fired back.

Safra took a step back in surprise. She had thought of
Meera as a gentle and kind woman who never sneered or
shouted. "Yikes. I've never seen Mother like that," Raisha
whispered.

The Captain shivered. "Yikes is the word."

"I want my Scepter," Neera demanded.

"You will not get it!" Meera said.

"Oh no! The Scepter is in the cave!" Ahmed whispered.
"She could find it any time!" "Shhhh," Safra said.

"Well, I know you know where it is. You will give it to
me." Neera said.

"And if I don't?"

"I will fight you for it, with a sword."

"I would rather do that."

"All right, we can do it the hard way!" Neera whipped
out a black and silver sword.

Meera gasped. "Father's gift to you! You dare fight me with it?!"

"Of course!" Neera slashed at her playfully.

"Grrr," Meera growled, and twisted her hands together to create a sword made out of sparkling white light. They ran at each other, and their swords clashed.

"Wow. That woman can wield a sword!" The Captain said.

Safra stared at Meera, who had complete control over her sword, but was faltering. Neera kept attacking relentlessly, and did not let Meera take any advantage of the situation.

Safra could also see that Raisha was also worried. She kept whispering to herself and biting her nails.

"Arrrrgggghh!" Meera had lost her temper. Instead of blocking, she swung her sword at Neera, who tried to dodge by bending her head, but fell with a thud to the ground.

Meera let out a deep breath. She held her sword to Neera's throat.

"I give up," Neera dropped her sword and held up her hands in surrender.

"Humph!" Meera turned away from her. "I can't believe I'm sparing you!" She began to mutter to herself.

The two sisters did not speak. Meera sighed and sat down on a rock. Neera, who was behind her, did the same.

Safra was itching to come out of hiding and confront the both of them, but she stayed put, knowing that Neera could kill her if she had the chance.

They began to talk to each other, but in hushed voices. Safra strained her ear, but she could not hear them.

"No!" Meera shouted angrily, her back still turned away from Neera. "Never!"

"You don't understand. I am sorry."

Meera looked surprised, but did not have any response. Neera hung her head, but as Safra squinted, she could see that her eyes were scanning the landscape.

It all happened in a flash of a second. Neera grabbed her sword, and quickly slashed Meera's arm, leaving a large wound. She fell to the ground, clutching it tightly.

"Now you can't fight, can you? Ha!" Neera laughed and slashed Meera's leg as well! Red stained the fabric, quickly spreading.

"Mother!" Raisha clapped a hand over her mouth in shock.

The rest of them gasped.

SIXTY-TWO

THE PLAN

"Okay, we need a safer place to hide," Safra said. "Let's go behind the cave."

They crouched down behind some rocks. There were no hyenas in sight.

"Okay, we need a plan," Safra said.

"I have an idea," Raisha said, wiping her tears. "And I need you guys to distract Neera."

"Okay," the Captain said nervously.

"Sneak up behind her, and do something to make sure she won't see me."

"What exactly are you going to do?" Chuck asked.

"I'm going to try to take Mother to safety, maybe behind the cave, right here," Raisha said. "I'm going to try." "All right. Good luck," Safra said. "Come on guys," she said. They snuck to the other side of the cave, until they were behind Neera.

She raised her sword, ready to put an end to Meera.

She swung it.

Their hair stood on end. Dayak gasped. "She won't make it!"

But Neera stopped. "Don't worry. All I need is *ze* location of the Rose Scepter!"

"I…Won't…Tell…" Meera stammered in pain. "That's our cue!" Safra took out her bow and arrow. "Hey old lady!" Ridan taunted.

"You…You little troublemakers!" Neera lunged for Ridan. He stepped out of the way.

Safra fired an arrow, but missed. Neera swung at her, and the Captain blocked with his sword.

Safra peeked over his shoulder to see Raisha trying to help Meera up. She shook her head. "Too heavy," she mouthed to Safra.

"Do something, anything," she mouthed back.

Raisha looked around. There was no driftwood to use as a cane or a splint. She looked at a tree, a single leaf hanging from it. She curled her hands into fists, green light glowing from her locket. It began to blink rapidly. She looked at the tree, where a silver fox stood. It nodded at her.

She placed her hands over Meera's arm. The green light began to glow brighter. She tried with all her might, and did not dare to look. Soon the light faded.

Meera wriggled her arm from side to side. The wound had disappeared.

"I am so proud of you," she whispered.

"Stay still," Raisha, concentrating said as she did the same to her leg, happy tears welling in her eyes. "Be quiet."

Neera was still quite busy fighting them to notice. Safra let out a sigh of relief as Meera stood up and picked up her sword.

Raisha barreled into Neera and rolled away just in time. Meera knocked her sword out of her hand and quickly pinned her to the ground.

"I...I won't hesitate to hurt you this time!" Her eyes glowed with anger.

Neera remained silent. "Tie her up," the Captain ordered them. Chuck and Ahmed did as they were told.

"Ridan, Safra, find the other Hunters," he said. "Aye aye, Captain!" Safra smiled and saluted. They hurried off.

As she ran, she glanced at Raisha, who was staring at her hands. "I actually did that. I actually did that," she whispered to herself. She caught Safra's gaze, who nodded and disappeared.

"The Hunters and the boat are gone!" Ridan reported. "What? Really?" Safra checked as well, but no avail.

The Captain rushed to the scene.

"They must have fled. We can worry about that later," he said.

Chuck and Ahmed had tied Neera to a rock.

"I must thank you all profusely," Meera said. "And I must repay you."

"You already have," the Captain jingled the key to the silver sand.

"So be it. I shall take you to the sand, and then back to your shipmates." Safra noticed that Meera was holding the Scepter.

"I cannot describe how brave you all have been." "It's all thanks to Safra and Ridan," the Captain said. Safra blushed and pushed her fingers into her pockets, but something did not feel right.

"Ridan! Where's that extra locket that we made?" she asked quickly.

"You had it," he answered.

"But it's gone," she said, and turned. Her eyes widened in alarm.

"Neera's gone!" In the distance, a black boat disappeared, turning away from Silver Island.

"With the locket! The Hunters must have taken her with them!" Safra said.

"Do not worry; it was not a very powerful locket. She can only grow plants," Raisha explained.

"I do not know what she will do with it, but that is not a worry for us now. She has left Silver Island, and that is enough. Now, we must take you to the volcano."

SIXTY-THREE

THE MONA—AGAIN

Meera had made a huge whirlwind that transported them back to the volcano. Then, she whispered something into Dayak's ear, and he flew off.

At the look of their confused faces, she explained, "After Neera became my enemy, I told my followers and members of my court of a hiding place to use if she ever managed to conquer us. Then, I was cursed."

"Then, I was imprisoned, and everyone fearfully hid," Raisha said.

"All but one."

Safra immediately recognized the voice.

"Zelda, my dear friend!" The two women hugged. Zelda smiled and brushed fur off her dress. Silver fur.

"You…You were the silver fox!" Safra burst out loud. She laughed and nodded, and Raisha joined in on the hug.

"Well, now it's our moment," the Captain said. "We'll leave them to their reunion." He took a deep breath and took out the key.

"Hello, Guardian!" Safra said cheerily.

"You have gotten the key! That means…" He rushed outside. "My queen!"

"All of us shall do the honors. This is it," Ahmed said. They inserted the key into the hole.

They took a deep breath, and turned it, all of their hands on the key. It clicked, and then, the door opened.

They gasped. Bright light hit them like a bullet. Finally, as it faded, they could see the wonderful things that they had done all of this for.

Sparkly, silver mounds of sand were piled everywhere. Safra leaped into one.

"This is my life's work!" The Captain fell on his knees.

"Come and jump in!" Safra spat out some out of the sand on the ground.

"How are you going to take all of it? Weren't there any consequences?" Ahmed said.

"Don't be silly." The Captain said. He reached into his coat and took out a small bottle. He slowly shifted some of the sand into it. "That should be enough," he murmured.

"Captain? Are you crazy? We came all this way, and we find something that's magical, and that's all you take?"

"I'm not planning to use it," the Captain said, smiling. "I'm happy enough keeping it in a museum or something."

He winked at Safra, who smiled. He *had* changed.

Ahmed looked very confused.

Ridan was swimming happily in the sand. "Let's take a little bit for Grandpa! He'll be so proud!"

"But…"

The Captain held out another bottle. "Use this," he told Safra. She filled it unto the brim with the sand.

She felt an unusual sense of happiness. Her heart felt
light, like it could just leap out of her mouth. She felt like
she could just scream forever!

"Let's go home, shall we?" The Captain smiled. He
raised his bottle. "Don't worry all of you, this time the
credit will go to all of us!"

"Hooray!" They cheered.

They walked out of the volcano, heads held high, smiling
ear to ear.

"I can see that you are ready to go and join your
shipmates." Meera smiled. "I have a surprise— Dayak has
rescued your friends."

The Captain sighed in relief. "Come. We shall go."

SIXTY-FOUR

HOME SWEET HOME

They were back to the camp, after tearful goodbyes.
It was still a sweet reunion. The Captain was smiling and
hugging all of his crew, and laughing and talking.
 "I regret that I did not come with you," Jorge said. He
apologized to Chuck. "You are a man of great bravery,"
he said. "You have become one after this journey."
Chuck smiled.
 They are going to be good friends, Safra thought.
 Everything had been packed back onto the ship, and all
of them had boarded.
 "Ah, it feels so good to be behind the helm again," The
Captain said. A few days of traveling passed.
 "I wonder when the Ships will come to Erina again,"
Safra thought aloud.
 "We will be staying there until we get another
adventure," the Captain said. "Look, it's in sight!"
 "Oh, well that's surprising!" Safra said.
 Safra sat on the figurehead. She breathed in the air. It
had never felt so good to be alive!

She stared at the bright blue sea. A bright orange tail flipped in the water. Faro! He had escaped!

She looked around. The Captain and Ahmed had rekindled their friendship; Chuck had overcome his fears, and was now recognized. Ahmed had learnt to trust. The Captain had turned from a coward to a trustworthy mentor, and Safra had learned how to take failure. Ridan had found out that if he chased his dreams, they could come true, and Raisha had gained confidence in herself and her abilities. Their dreams had come true.

She imagined her grandfather, staring proudly at her. Tears of happiness welled in her eyes.

"Is everything okay, Safra?" Ridan asked.

"Perfect." She stared at the island of Erina. It had never felt this good to be home.

ACKNOWLEDGEMENTS

First of all, I would love to thank my parents for their wonderful support. First to my Mom, who taught me at home every single day, and then to Dad, who encouraged me to write every day, and he was also a wonderful editor. Next I would thank my twin sister, Bharathi, and my best friend Maddox Nowak for being a big part of my writing journey. You guys make my day feel special. Also, I could not have done this without my piano teacher, Miss Stefanie Rittner, who read all my writing and supported me, and to my art teacher, Mrs. Debbie Howard, whose teaching helped me create this book's illustrations. Finally, I would like to thanks authors around the world, who inspired me to read and write.
 I thank all of you with all my heart, and that is the most difficult thing I cannot convey enough in my words.

Yours lovingly,
Vaanathi

ABOUT THE AUTHOR

Vaanathi Chonachalam is a thirteen-year-old girl who has loved writing since she was seven years old. She started out with one-page stories, and now this is her first novel. When she's not writing a novel, she's usually editing one or thinking of more ideas for her next one.